ROBIN HOOD

AND HIS MERRIE MEN

DEAN

This edition published 1992 by Dean,
part of Reed International Books Ltd.,
Michelin House, 81 Fulham Road, London SW3 6RB

This edition first published 1957 by Dean & Son Ltd.

ISBN 0 603 55068 1

Printed and bound in Italy by OFSA S.p.A.

ROBIN HOOD
HOOD

AND HIS MERRIE MEN

CONTENTS

6 CONTENTS

CHAPTER I

GREENWOOD DREAMS

"MOTHER!" called a small lad, as he came into the house after a morning's wandering in the forest. "Is dinner ready?"

"Yes, Robin," came his mother's reply from the kitchen.

Dinner was already on the table when Robin walked into the kitchen. He sat at the rough wooden table and started to eat.

Afterwards, when Robin's mother was washing up the dishes, the boy sat for a time gazing out through the open doorway into the depths of the greenwood.

"Mother," he said, suddenly, "is it true that Sir Guy of Coventry was your uncle?"

"Why, yes, Robin," was the answer. "Who told you?"

Robin walked into the kitchen and picked up a cloth to dry the dishes with.

"And is it true that he killed the wild boar by himself?" he went on.

"Yes, he did," laughed his mother. "It was a very brave deed, Robin."

"Tell me about it, Mother," asked Robin.

The good woman, who was dressed in a long blue gown, drew up the footstool on the rush-covered floor of the kitchen, and told her son the story of Sir Guy's deed. Robin sat by her, listening intently.

Sir Guy had set out into the forest to attack, single-handed, the wild blue boar that had killed several countrymen as they passed through the forest. Alone, Sir Guy had trapped the beast and plunged a long knife into its heart. Then he had carried home its grizzly head, with its enormous tusks, as a trophy.

Robin sat for a time, picturing again his brave ancestor going alone into the forest, knife in hand.

"It's not like you to miss the afternoon sunshine, Robin," his mother said, as she picked up a pail to fill it from a nearby brook.

"No, Mother, but I was just thinking." He stood up and picked from his worn hose bits of rush that had clung to him as he sat on the floor. " There are still wild boars in the forest, aren't there?"

"Yes, but not so dangerous as the beast killed by Sir Guy of Coventry," explained his mother.

Robin walked down the grassy path that led from the cottage, and was soon happily skipping through the belt of trees that marked the edge of Sherwood Forest.

Tea-time passed in Robin's home with no sign of the boy. His mother, well used to her son's ways, saved his tea for him and began to prepare a meal for her husband on his return from work. But when the sun had gone slowly to rest and the old oil-lamps had been lit to brighten the dark cottage there was great anxiety about Robin's safety.

His father decided to search for the boy, and he was setting out towards the dark shapes of the trees when he saw a figure running towards the house. It was Robin.

"Where have you been?" stormed his father. His voice brought Robin's mother to the door.

Robin's clothing was torn and dirty. He went to his mother. She held him tightly.

"Answer my question! Where have you been?" thundered his father, eyeing a riding-whip that was hanging on the cottage wall.

"I—I went deep into the forest to see if I could find a wild boar. I meant to slay him, as Sir Guy did!"

"It is lucky for you that you didn't find one," said his father. He led them back into the house. "But," he continued, his rage calming as quickly as it had risen, "it was brave of you to go and seek the boar. It is lucky for you and for us who love you that you did not come up with him."

"All the same, it was exciting," said Robin. "I met a crowd of rough men, who wanted to know how I came there. And when I told them they laughed at me."

"You are but a boy," said his father gently.

"Then they gave me something to eat and drink," went on Robin; "and they said that perhaps one day I should find a home in the forest myself."

"Heaven forbid!" cried his mother. She hurriedly brought him the tea she had saved.

"It must be a fine life," said Robin, almost to himself. "Imagine sleeping in the forest, and living in the open-air all day long!"

As Robin lay on his rough wood bed, watching the rising moon as it sent silvery glimmers through the breeze-blown leaves outside his room, he wondered how he could ever settle down to learning a trade when the greenwood around him offered a life of freedom and adventure.

Through the years, while he was growing from a boy into sturdy manhood, Robin never forgot that first adventure in the forest. He spent his leisure time wrestling, leaping, and running with the other boys. He learnt to fight with big poles, called quarter-staffs, and with great sticks with handles like baskets, with which two fighters tried to crack each other's heads. He became quite at home on the back of a horse, learning to set it at high fences, and leap them. But his favourite sport was with his bow-and-arrows, aiming at a target.

So he grew up, a manly, robust young fellow, who could run swiftly, ride with great skill, wing an arrow true to its target, and fight bravely with his fists or with staves.

CHAPTER 2

THROUGH THE GREENWOOD

As ROBIN grew from boy to youth, his father thought seriously about his son's future. It was time that the lad learned a trade. His great strength suited him to many trades, but his adventurous, high-spirited nature caused his father some worry.

Nevertheless, Robin's mother and father were very proud of their daring young son. Sturdy, well built, handsome, and full of fun and good humour, he was popular amongst his friends.

In far-away Nottingham, Robin's mother had a brother. He was Squire Gamwell of Gamwell Hall, a good man, fond of youngsters, and ever ready to give a helping hand to those in need. Robin's mother had not seen him for many years, and she wanted very much to show her sturdy young son to him.

"My lord," she said one day to her husband, "it is some years since I saw my brother. Would it not be possible for me to go to Nottingham to visit him?"

Her husband thought deeply.

"I would love you to go, my dear," he said at length. "But there are difficulties in the way. You see, it means in the first place that someone would have to go with you. You cannot, of course, go alone."

"I realise that," agreed his wife. "Someone would have to protect me from the bands of robbers along the road."

"Yes, and you realise, too, that I cannot possibly go myself," went on her husband. "I cannot afford the time for such a long journey. The trouble is that I can think of nobody who could undertake the trip."

His wife sat silent for a few moments. She was not surprised at her husband's reply. She had expected something like that. Now was the time to bring out the secret hope that she had in her mind.

"Could I not take Robin?" she begged, eagerly, trying at the same time to make the remark sound casual. "He is strong enough to protect me." Then she added, confidently, "Though it is a forty-mile journey, I know I shall be safe with him."

Her husband gave a merry laugh.

"I understand perfectly," he chuckled. "The hen wants to show off her sturdy young chicken."

He was silent again. He considered deeply. Could he rely upon his son to defend his mother? The lad was certainly strong enough to cope with possible danger. His next remark settled the question.

"You want your brother to see our manly son," he said. "Very natural, too. Take the lad, my dear; and I shall be glad to know how your brother is."

Robin's mother was almost beside herself with happiness. She could hardly wait to find Robin and to tell him the news. She ran through the open door of the cottage and found him walking towards her.

"Robin!" she exclaimed, excitedly. "We are going to Nottingham!"

"To Nottingham!" echoed Robin.

"Just you and me," went on his mother.

"Oh, Mother!" laughed Robin. "That will be wonderful. When are we going?"

Robin was all excited now, but there was a great deal of preparation necessary before they could start out on the long journey. With no means of travelling except by horse, they had to make sure that there was enough food and drink to last the journey. Then Robin was given a new set of clothes. The horse's shoes were examined, the bridle cleaned, and the saddle made as comfortable as possible.

"Come here, son," said Robin's father, "and I'll draw you a map of the route you must take."

Robin listened carefully while his father explained in great detail the roads he must follow, where he was most likely to meet robbers, and where he could leave the road and take short cuts through forest-land.

At last all plans were completed. The water-bottles were filled, and the horse was loaded for the journey.

"You have a grand day to start the journey off," said Robin's father as he stood gazing at the clear blue sky.

Dressed in her gayest holiday clothes, Robin's mother came into the yard where Robin, with his horse, awaited her. His father had bought him a sword, which he now wore proudly, and in his belt was thrust a dagger.

Robin sprang lightly into the saddle, and waited while his mother was lifted into the pillion behind him.

"Good luck go with you!" called his father as, on the one horse, the two set out on their forty-mile journey.

It was slow travelling; the horse ambled along through the great forest. Soon they were on the great road that led to Nottingham. For mile upon mile they met nobody, but when they had left the cottage many miles behind, and were making slow progress along the road, they saw two men coming towards them.

Robin jumped off his horse, held the reins in his left hand, and gripped his sword with his right. But the men were peaceful travellers, and they passed by with a friendly greeting.

After travelling many more miles along the open, dusty, sun-baked road, Robin and his mother reached Nottingham at last. From the town to Gamwell Hall was only a short ride.

Robin's uncle was pleased to see him when he arrived.

"So this is my nephew!" he laughed, as he helped Robin's mother down from the horse. He could see that the lad was well built and intelligent. When he had embraced Robin's mother, he turned. "Hey, Will!" he called, shouting into the old Hall. "Come and meet your cousin!"

Will Gamwell came to the door. He was a tall, fair-haired youth, about the same age as Robin. The two became friends at once.

"We'll have some fun tomorrow," said Robin's uncle, when they were seated round the table for a meal. "We must see what stuff you are made of."

"I can hardly wait for tomorrow to come," confided Robin to his mother when at last they were alone together. "I have a feeling that something exciting is about to happen."

CHAPTER 3

TRIALS OF STRENGTH

ROBIN was awake early the next morning. He was rested after his long journey and was soon springing lightly down the long staircase of Gamwell Hall to where his cousin, Will, was at breakfast.

"Good morning, Will!" said Robin.

"Hallo, Robin!" returned Will, with a smile. "I've got some dull news for you."

"What's that?" asked Robin. He sat down at the table.

"My cousin is coming to stay here for a week!"

"What's dull about that?" asked Robin. "He might be good fun."

"It isn't a he; it's a she!"

"Oh!" said Robin.

That was different. Boys were usually good fun, but girls were so soft, and they played such silly games.

Yet, in spite of himself, Robin could not help liking Maid Marian when he met her later that morning. She was pretty and ladylike, it was true, but she had also an imp of mischief in her eyes and liked to take part in all the boys' games. She could outpace many of the boys in running, and she was no mean marks-woman with the bow-and-arrow. Robin liked her from the first.

Squire Gamwell held a great feast at Gamwell Hall, and he invited all the villagers from round about as well as his large number of friends from outlying districts.

The guests had a jolly time, and the merry peals of laughter rang out until they could be heard far away from the estate.

A great meal was prepared and set out on the long trestle-tables that were placed round the Hall. And afterwards, when everyone had eaten their fill, the Squire suggested that all the guests should go to the lawn, where some sports would be held. The guests soon made a large semi-circle on the grass.

"We need a Queen of Ceremonies!" cried one of

the party, and his cry was taken up by all the young folk present.

There was no question as to who would be made Queen, for Maid Marian was without doubt the most beautiful young lady present at the gathering. She was soon brought forward and crowned Queen. Squire Gamwell placed a seat on a table, and Maid Marian was hoisted up to her throne.

"As Queen of Ceremonies," she announced, with a smile, "I command that the young men shall match their strength against one another."

Robin was excited about the challenge thrown out. He had practised hard at all the boys' sports of the day with youngsters from his own district. And, though he was a stranger here, he was determined to show his skill to the lovely Maid Marian.

He knew that he was matched against rivals who were really experienced at the art of quarter-staff fighting. However, he fought bravely and fiercely. His youthful training was useful to him, and he found himself winning against each contestant. Robin was as pleased as they were surprised. His quarter-staff whirled about their heads more quickly than did their staffs; and when his staff struck his opponent's, Robin's strength was such that the staff was driven out of the rival's hands.

Maid Marian was delighted with her friend's skill. She watched with pride as next Robin was matched against the young men with swords. It was no match at all; Robin was quicker on his feet than they were. The young men fought hard to win the contest, for they felt annoyed that this unknown youth should be so much better than they. Their efforts were not enough, however, and Robin won every contest.

"Bravo!" cried the Queen of Ceremonies.

It was Marian's only wish now that Robin should win the final series of contests—with the bow-and-arrows. She felt sure that he would beat all rivals, but Squire Gamwell, knowing how skilful were the other young men at this sport, had little hope that his brave young nephew would put up much of a show as an archer.

"He's got the strength of a man in his young body," whispered the Squire to Robin's mother as they watched the contest. "But it's something more than strength that is wanted with the bow. It's a good eye and a steady aim."

At last came the trial. When Robin's turn came he put into use all that he had learned from his continual practice, ever since, as a boy, he had been inspired by the tale of Sir Guy and the wild boar.

Robin's arrow went straight to the centre of the target. Yet his was not the only arrow that went quivering to the mark. One or two of the other fellows were skilful enough to score a bull's-eye. There had to be some other way to decide the winner. The youths appealed to Maid Marian to suggest how the winner should be selected.

Robin came to the rescue with an idea. He ran to Maid Marian and whispered it into her ear.

"That is a fine idea, Robin," she said, as he jumped down from the table. She turned to the crowd. "I command that a slender willow-rod shall be placed in the ground, and anyone who can hit it with his arrow from forty paces shall be the winner."

The youths stood looking on while Robin fixed up the rod. Some of them laughed.

"What? Why, it would be impossible to hit that!" one cried. All the young men agreed.

"Then watch this!" said Robin.

He drew his bow, and, taking careful aim, he shot his arrow. The whole gathering was breathlessly silent. All eyes were turned towards the slender rod of willow.

Crack!

The willow-rod was split in two as the arrow from Robin's bow pierced it. A roar of applause went up.

Robin's mother was proud of her son that day, but Maid Marian was even more thrilled at the skill of her new-found friend.

CHAPTER 4

ESCAPE FROM PRISON

ROBIN and his mother stayed with Squire Gamwell for more than a week. They would have stayed longer, but an unexpected adventure cut short their visit and caused them to return home in haste.

During the few days after the great feast at Gamwell Hall, Robin quickly became a great favourite with the village folk. He was the leader in all manner of fun and mischief. Squire Gamwell thought that Robin's apparent wildness was due to his having lived such a quiet life. But Robin's mother knew that there was a spirit of adventure in her son that could not be quenched.

Maid Marian was often at Robin's side. She, too, stayed a week with her uncle. While Robin and she were together, they shared their fun happily.

" We must not miss the fair!" shouted Robin, as he ran into the Hall.

He and Marian had heard the news that was going round the village that the annual fair would be held in Nottingham that day.

"You'll get a poor welcome from the townspeople," warned Will Gamwell. "Every year we go to the fair, and every year the same thing happens. The stupid people of Nottingham look down on people from the villages, like us, and there's usually trouble."

"We'll give them trouble this year, all right!" laughed Robin.

A party of youths, headed by Robin and Marian, walked into Nottingham when the fair was in full swing. The tradespeople, behind their brightly coloured stalls, took no notice of the band of villagers. But groups of youths from Nottingham soon spotted them and before long started to hurl insults at Robin and his friends.

It was a new experience for Robin to see a fair, and he ignored the insults while he watched keenly all that was going on. But the townsfolk began to jeer at them. Robin was too spirited to suffer this without answer.

"Over with the stalls, comrades!"

Three of the stalls were overturned before the townsfolk realised fully what was happening. The next moment a cry was set up for help. The townsfolk, armed with staves, tried to rush Robin's band, but Robin leapt into the fray and fought back daringly.

"Take that!" he yelled, as he closed in on one burly fellow. "Show them what village lads are made of!"

Robin stayed right in the thick of the fighting.

Then, as if they had seen a ghost, most of the townspeople suddenly stopped fighting and fled in the opposite direction. It wasn't a ghost they had seen. It was the Sheriff. He was riding into the fairground with a strong force of guards.

"Robin! Robin! Come away!" yelled his friends.

But Robin was too busy with the last of the townspeople to heed.

"Get that man!" roared the Sheriff, espying Robin as he sent another man crashing to the ground.

The Sheriff's men rushed at Robin. He was overwhelmed and carried, struggling gamely, to the Sheriff.

"You've killed a man, you young law-breaker!" stormed the Sheriff. "You'll be charged with that crime." He turned to his men. "Take him away. Throw him into prison!"

Robin had no chance against so many of the Sheriff's guards. He was dragged to the town prison and flung into an empty cell.

"I wonder if Maid Marian escaped?" was Robin's first thought as he sat on the straw of the prison cell.

Soon he began to look about him. The cell was about eight feet square. Like all prisons in his time, this one was made of timber, with a small opening near the roof to allow of light filtering into the place. As he looked up, Robin saw that the dungeon was old, and that there were great holes in the ceiling. Through these holes he could see the straw-thatched roof.

"If I can't get out of this place I'm a duffer!" said he to himself.

When darkness fell, Robin climbed to the roof of the prison and broke through the thatching. It was an easy matter for him to force his way to the outside of the roof and then to slide down to the ground.

"Take him, dead or alive!" ordered the Sheriff when he heard the news of Robin's escape.

Robin hurried back to his uncle's house. He bade a sad farewell to Maid Marian, placed his mother on his horse, and rode back with her over the forty-mile route by which they had come. All the time his thoughts dwelt on the injustice of being cast into prison for something he had not done.

He reached home at last, but he could not rest long, for news followed swiftly that the Sheriff's men were seeking him. He wanted desperately to avoid bringing his father into conflict with the Sheriff. He knew he must leave home.

"My father shall not be mixed up in this," he vowed to himself. "Until the hue and cry has quietened down, I must hide in the forest."

Robin went that day. His exciting adventures as an outlaw were beginning.

CHAPTER 5

"ROBIN HOOD, DEAD OR ALIVE!"

IT WAS noon next day when the Sheriff's men arrived at the house where Robin's uncle lived.

"I demand that you hand over Robin Hood in the name of His Majesty the King!" ordered the leader.

"Robin Hood left for home yesterday," answered Squire Gamwell. "He lives forty miles away!"

Forty miles did not deter the Sheriff's men. After their orders from the Sheriff they dared not return without bringing back their prisoner.

"Get me Robin Hood, dead or alive!" the Sheriff had commanded early that morning. "Am I to be made a fool of in my own town? Is it to be known that a man can break out of my own gaol? Am I not answerable to the King himself for the punishment of those who offend against the laws of the country? Bring me Robin Hood, I say! Get him—dead or alive!"

When the Sheriff's men had covered the forty miles to the cottage where Robin lived, they were met by Robin's father.

"We have orders to arrest Robin Hood," said the leader. "We demand, in the name of His Majesty the King, that you hand him over to us."

"He is not here," replied Robin's father. "He is in the forest. If you venture through, take great care.

Anybody who goes along the forest-paths makes an excellent target for the arrows of men who are skilled with the bow. Some of you may never see Nottingham again if you do not take care."

In spite of any wrong that his son had done, Robin's father was trying to protect him by dissuading the Sheriff's men from going into the forest.

The Sheriff's men listened to him; but they searched the house and grounds just the same, in case the lad was hiding there all the time.

"He's spoken the truth, all right," said the leader. "We shall have to seek Robin Hood in the forest." There was disappointment in his voice; he and his men were going to face a search that was not pleasant.

At the edge of the forest they halted. They realised how futile it would be to try to march through the undergrowth when behind every tree and bush a hidden marksman might be waiting. The Sheriff's men turned and took the winding road to Nottingham. It was safer!

Robin had entered the forest in the evening time, and he wandered through the quiet glades, trying to decide what would be best for him to do.

"Yet, this is the life I have longed for!" he murmured to himself. "This is the free, open-air life for which I have yearned!"

He gathered a heap of leaves and brushwood; then, with his flint and steel, he made a spark and let it fall on a piece of tinder-wood that he kept in his box. Placing the smouldering tinder in the heap of dry leaves, he blew into the flame, and soon had a bright fire burning.

Robin already felt lonely. Yet he was not alone. All his movements had been watched. The distant glow of the fire had been noticed by other outlaws. They had been in the forest a long time. Stealthily they gathered around him, creeping closer and closer.

Robin wrapped himself in his cloak and threw himself down to sleep. No sooner was he off his guard than the outlaws rushed at him. Robin stirred, to find himself surrounded by rough men.

"What d'you think you're doing?" demanded one of them.

"Who are you?" asked another.

Robin was wide awake by this time. He sat up and looked at the men around him.

"I am here because a certain gentleman, whom we call the Sheriff, invited me to be his guest in Nottingham," he told them. "He would hear of no refusal —he even sent a jolly band of men to escort me to him."

The men laughed.

"Did you go?" asked one.

"No! I came to the forest instead. I was told that the Sheriff was so keen to see me that he didn't care whether I was alive or dead! He'll never take me alive; and, as I don't want to die, I have changed my address. That's why I came—and I am here to stay."

The men smiled at his humour, and let him stay. They invited him to eat with them.

"We live on the King's deer, and the venison from it; there are birds in the trees that can also be shot and cooked."

So Robin joined the men, and found himself one of a band.

The story of his escape into the forest was talked

about in all the villages on that side of the forest where he used to live. It spread, too, around the villages on that side of the forest where his uncle's home was, at Gamwell Hall. They remembered with pride the talented youngster who had been with them for only a short time, and who had shown them how wonderfully skilled in manly sport he was.

When the harsh feudal laws of the day oppressed the homes of any of these villagers they would not hesitate to join Robin in the forest. One after another they came, and it was not long before a large number had joined the band. Those outlaws who were in the forest before Robin felt sure that one with so many friends and followers must surely be an important person. They were convinced that he was a man of much higher birth than themselves.

So he was. But he never boasted about the fact that his father was related to a very noble family, or that, had it not been for strange twists of fortune in relation to his mother's ancestors—the death of someone here, the marriage of someone there—he would have become Earl of Huntingdon.

After a while everyone began to look upon Robin as their natural leader. Not only did he come of good family, but he was superior to all in his use of the quarter-staff and sword, and, above all, of the bow-and-arrow.

By common consent he was made the outlaws' captain.

"We must have only the best of bows, made of strong, pliable yew," said Robin when all his band were seated round the camp-fire one night. "Our arrows, too, must be perfectly made."

He gave a great deal of time to making his band proficient with their weapons and useful with their fists. He thought it advisable for his men to carry, besides their arrows, short swords.

"And what about clothing?" he asked on one occasion. "It is fitting that we should be clad like men of the forest."

The outlaws were dressed at that time in many-coloured clothes, shabby and torn through much hard wear.

"Why not dress ourselves in green cloth?" Robin said. "Then, since the grass and the leaves of the forest are green, we should be less likely to be noticed."

All agreed that this was a fine idea.

Later Robin showed the men how by blowing different ways upon his horn, various messages could be sent. A number of sharp blasts could mean a cry for help; the sounding of two notes in quick succession could mean someone was calling; three sharp blasts could mean that Robin himself wanted to speak to his men.

It was early one summer evening when Robin called his followers about him.

"I have called you here," he said, "to tell you details of a great plan. It is useless for us to hide here as if we were all villains. We are living in strange times, where there seems to be one law for the rich and another for the poor. The rich are well looked after, whereas the poor are not only neglected but are treated worse than dogs. The barons in their castles do as they like. Let us teach them to do what *we* like!"

His men roared with laughter.

"You may well laugh!" said Robin. "There are a hundred and forty of us—as good men as ever drew a bow. Outside the forest there are many bad men, bad things, bad ways. Let us go and alter them! Let us right the wrongs done to the poor. Pledge me your word that our plan will be to help the poor!"

They agreed wholeheartedly with Robin's brave and chivalrous purpose. They pledged their word to support him.

CHAPTER 6

LITTLE JOHN

IN HIS new suit of Lincoln green, Robin strolled round the outlaw camp in Sherwood Forest. He watched his men preparing arrows, refixing bow-strings, and carrying out sundry repairs to their weapons.

"They look as if they are fresh from battle," mused Robin to himself. "Yet for two weeks little has happened in the way of adventure."

Robin felt restless about the future. He spoke to Much-the-Miller's son, one of the new members of the band.

"It's all very well to be the leader of so fine a band of men—and the band is still growing—but what's the use of trained fighting men if you can give them no work to do?"

The burly miller's son laid his hand on the leader's arm.

"Don't worry, master," he said. "We are contented. After all, this is the life we chose."

But Robin Hood was restive, athirst for action.

"It's no good waiting here in the forest for some adventure to come along. It's getting dull here. I must go outside and look for something more exciting."

He set out later in the day, alone. He reminded his men to keep their ears sharpened for the call of his horn should there be trouble. Through the greenwood he wandered, making his way over tangled undergrowth until he came to one of the shady forest paths. Along the path, aimlessly, he walked until he came to a second path that led across the fields to a distant village.

To his left ran a stream, and he followed it for some way as it threaded a wavy course through the fields. Presently he came to a roughly made wooden bridge. He mounted the bridge, but there he came to a sudden halt. Standing at the opposite end of the bridge was a giant of a man. He had started to cross at the same time as the outlaw.

Robin walked along the bridge to where the stranger stood. The giant made no attempt to let him pass. Instead he stood squarely in the middle of the bridge and glared insolently at Robin, as if daring him to try to pass.

Here was a situation that promised some excitement. Robin laughed merrily. It was clear that the stranger had no intention of letting him pass. Yet one of them must retreat before the other could cross—and Robin Hood, leader of the Sherwood

Forest outlaws, had no intention of giving way to a stranger, however big he might be.

Robin glanced at the swirling stream below. His mind was made up.

"Let me pass, fellow!" he commanded.

The huge man did not move.

"If you don't move out of my way, you great oaf, I shall have to move you myself!" cried Robin.

The fellow only grinned. Robin became infuriated. He unslung his bow.

"If you don't move," he warned, "I'll show you how we deal with fellows like you."

As Robin fitted an arrow to his bow, the giant lumbered forward towards him. Poised in his hands was a quarter-staff.

"If you dare pull back the string," he said, grimly, "I'll dust the hide off you."

They were brave words, for Robin, with his bow, had the advantage. Robin could have killed him if he had chosen. There was no denying this great fellow's courage as he stared scornfully at the threatening bow. Robin admired his spirit. The outlaw backed slightly to the end of the footbridge, still with his arrow pointing certain death at the stranger.

"Your talk is foolish," said he. "I could send an arrow through your heart in quicker time than it would take to tell."

"You are a coward!" exclaimed the other, with scorn in his voice. "You are armed with bow-and-arrows; I have only my stout staff."

"Coward!" laughed Robin. "I like that! I'll soon show you that I am no coward."

Robin leapt off the bridge and, going to a nearby

B

oak-tree, sprang at one of the branches. By sheer force he tore it down. Quickly he stripped off the leaves and ran back to the bridge.

In the middle of the bridge the two men met. They flourished their staves. Robin got in a blow on the giant's shoulder. Fighting back, the man hit Robin on the head with his staff. The fight grew furious. The two were well matched, for Robin was a practised fighter, and the stranger was enormously strong.

Robin rained in a shower of blows, thick and fast. The stranger smote back with a will. Then, just as Robin was beginning to think he was getting the upper hand, he missed his footing and fell with a great splash into the brook.

He struggled to the surface. Heavy rains had swollen the stream, and in the middle it was deep.

"Ho! Where are you now, my fine fellow?" laughed the stranger.

Robin spluttered from the water: "I'm in the flood. You proved yourself the better man that time."

"All right!" answered the other. "So long as you own you're beaten I'll let you cross the bridge."

Robin waded out, lower down the stream. He was muddy and wet. He came up to the stranger, and asked him what his business was and whether he had work to do. The giant shook his head.

"Nobody within miles will give John Little even a day's work," he said. "They're all afraid to employ me. The trouble is that I like to work in my own way. They all want me to work in their way. But nobody ever made John Little do what he didn't want to do—so it always ended in a fight and I had to wander on, often hungry. I could eat a good meal now!"

While the gaint was speaking, Robin had been trying to wash some of the mud from his new suit of Lincoln green.

"Come back with me," he said, picking up his bow and arrows. "I'll show you a band of fine fellows who would be glad to give you a good meal."

He turned back the same way as he had come, the stranger striding after him.

As the two reached Sherwood Forest, Robin grasped his horn and placed it to his lips. His only answer was a stream of dirty water that still lay in the instrument after its soaking in the brook. Robin laughed merrily, and his companion joined in.

Robin shook the horn dry and blew again. Three loud notes rang out through the greenwood. Other horns quickly answered his call, and soon a crowd of men, dressed like himself in Lincoln green, surrounded them.

Robin gazed at them proudly.

"These are my merry men, O John Little," he said. "And this," he continued, turning to his men, "is a man who would not let me pass across a bridge this morning, and instead tumbled me into a stream. What shall we do with him?"

"Duck him!" they cried. "Throw him into a stream as you were thrown!"

"No!" answered Robin. "He has proved himself a fighter with a staff. He had far better join us." He turned to the giant. "Come, join my merry band!" he said. "We have plenty to eat and drink, and as for the work we have to do—well, our work is to 'right the wrong'! If there is a tyrant anywhere

about, or if a man robs the poor, he has to settle
with us. There will be plenty of fighting. It is a
hard life, but it offers fine sport. What say you?"

John Little was keen to join. The band turned
back towards their camp, and when they reached
it Robin Hood, winking mischievously, said to his
merry men: "We shall have to re-christen him!"

The men laughed, and swarmed about John Little,
dragging him down to the ground. Will-the-Wrestler
suggested a new name.

"He says he's John Little. Then let us call him
'Little John'!"

They poured mugfuls of water over the giant, and
he became 'Little John' from that day forward.
They dressed him in their uniform of Lincoln green.
They taught him to shoot, and how to use his sword
and dagger. He never knew again what it was to be
hungry, for Robin Hood and his merry band of
outlaws dined richly off the King's deer, which they
shot in their forest-home.

Little John grew steadily in favour with the outlaws. His rough ways were understood by all, and
he became a great favourite. Robin often left him
in charge of the band while he went off by himself.
The men respected the giant, whose strength was
enormous, and they were satisfied to have one so
brave and strong as their leader when Robin was
away.

CHAPTER 7

THE OUTLAW CODE

PASSING one day through Sherwood Forest, a traveller was ambushed by Robin Hood's men, and captured. His hands were roughly thrust behind him,
and tied tightly.

"Well done!" said Little John. "We will take the
fellow to Robin Hood."

They wended their way through the forest, the
traveller with his bundles and his horse going in
front of them.

Robin Hood was angry when he examined the
traveller.

"Who tied this man's hands behind him in this
ruthless manner?" he demanded, turning upon his
men.

They looked at each other in surprise. Then Little
John said: "I did it! And I thought it very well
done!"

"You did!" said Robin, angrily. "I can see you
did!" He turned to his men. "Seize Little John and
tie him up in the same way!"

Despite his struggles, the giant was overpowered,
and his hands were tied tightly behind his back, as
he had tied those of the traveller. His bonds cut
deeply into his wrists. But the outlaws, though they
did as they were told, could not understand their

leader's purpose. There were some black looks for
him from a number of his band. The looks were
noted by Robin. He turned to Little John and said:
"Now, how do you like it yourself? Was it necessary to tie the captive's hands so tightly? It is un-
pleasant enough to be taken captive without adding
to a man's discomfort. Never tie too tightly, or I
shall tie you! Don't handle people too roughly, or I
shall see that you no longer remain men of my band.
I want strong men, it is true, but they must also be
men of gentle hearts."

Robin spoke directly to Little John.

"You have had your lesson, and now you shall be
freed, Little John. You and I know each other well,
and you will understand my rough handling. I did
it to show the rest how we must take prisoners."

When his thongs were removed Little John looked
ruefully at his wrists. He turned to the prisoner.

"I did not realise that I had tied you so tightly,"
he said. "Pray forgive me."

"Very handsomely said!" exclaimed Robin. "And
now"—turning to the captive traveller—"sit down on
the grass and tell us where you were taking your
goods, and from where you came."

His bonds cut, the man sat down.

"This morning," he began, "as the sun rose in the
heavens, I set forth from Nottingham with my goods.
You will see that I am only a young man. I have not
been in business long, and in Nottingham I found
it was slow work waiting for customers to come to
me. So I decided to pack my horse with some of my
coarser cloth and travel to the villages. I thought that
I might be able to sell some cloth to the labourers and
their women.

"But as I wandered along the forest path, your men surprised me and brought me here. It is a great pity that I did not know beforehand that I should fall into your hands, for I should certainly have brought some Lincoln-green cloth with me to sell to you."

Robin and his men burst out laughing at the way in which this man seemed to take for granted that he had missed a bargain.

"Then you were not travelling to sell some fine dainty cloths to the squires of the district and their ladies?" queried Robin.

"Certainly not," said the man. "Had I done so they might have taken what they wanted and left me to find the money as best I could; for we live in a time when might is right."

Robin nodded; he knew too well that this was the truth. He turned to his men.

"Open his pack," he said, "and if he has spoken the truth about his travelling to sell to honest poor folk he shall go on his way unmolested."

The pack was opened and it was found as the traveller had claimed, bales of russet-browns, and cloth of grey and drab, such as common folk would wear; but there was no cloth that any knight or dame or squire or lady would have dreamed of wearing.

"The man has spoken the truth!" declared Robin. "We have no wish to wage war upon the poor, and we don't want to spoil their chances of making an honest living. Let us, then, allow this man to go free. What do you say, men?"

The outlaws broke out into loud applause, and the traveller felt relieved to think that he was now a free man.

"I will ride this way again," he said; "and when I do I will bring with me some bales of Lincoln green. I should do a very good trade with you, for there are at least a hundred of you."

"You seem very sure that we should pay you for your goods!" said Little John.

"So sure," replied the traveller, "that it will not be long before you will see me again."

Robin gave the man a good meal of venison before he went on his way. When the travelling merchant arrived at the villages, he told the people how well Robin had treated him, and the reason why he was spared. Thus the villagers knew that Robin and his Merrie Men were their friends. Robin's own men, too, had been taught a valuable lesson that day—that they were not to harm the interests of the common folk.

The traveller was as good as his word. Not more than a week had gone by when he returned with his horse laden with cloth of Lincoln green. The outlaws paid him in full for his material, and he rode off well content.

Yet only a few days later he was back, and there was trouble written on his face.

"After I left you," he told Robin Hood, "I must have taken the wrong path near Nottingham, for in the dusk I was set upon by a band of robbers. The fiends took all my money and my horse. I was left there to find my own way home."

"Take us to the place where you went astray," said Robin.

Somewhat unwillingly, the man did so.

"I think it was here that I wandered off the right path," he said, after they had gone a long distance.

Robin and his Merrie Men searched thoroughly for signs of a struggle, but they could find none. Robin noted this and ordered his men to march the traveller back to their camp in the forest. Then Robin sent two of his men to visit the traveller's house and his shop in the town. He was suspicious about the truth of the story he had been told, but he gave no sign of this to the traveller.

"I'm afraid you will have to remain with us as our guest," said Robin, "until we can find out who stole your goods."

The man had no option but to stay, and it was not until late the following afternoon that Robin's messengers returned. As they came out of the forest into the camp-clearing, Robin, who had been waiting for them, went forward to meet them.

"The man has lied!" they said. "When we visited his stable we found, safely inside, the horse he told us had been stolen."

Robin had suspected as much. He was very angry. He strode over to the traveller.

"You are a fine trader," he said. "You thought to yourself, 'Robin Hood and his Merrie Men have good hearts. I will go and return to them, and tell them I have been robbed; and then perhaps they will give me money to help me.' It was your bad luck that you told me your horse was stolen, for my men found it at home in your stable."

The man trembled at these words.

"I am sorry, good master!" he cried. "Spare me! I will never cheat again!"

He was desperately afraid now that he was found out that his life would be forfeit.

Robin was silent for a moment. Then he said,

"You lied for money, and with money shall you pay your sentence. You will stay here until, at your own request, someone from your home shall bring a ransom. Every penny that you made from us when you sold us the cloth you must hand back. We only want your profits. We would not stoop to rob you of what the cloth actually cost you in the first place."

The wretched cheat had to agree. Robin's terms were carried out. A member of the traveller's family brought to Sherwood Forest the correct amount of money, and the traveller was then allowed to go home.

By this example, the justice that was in the mind of Robin Hood began to dawn on his Merrie Men. They began to understand that it was not Robin's intention to hurt ploughman or labourer. In fact, he had no wish to harm even a high-born knight who was honest and good. But if he knew of anyone cheating, or robbing, or lying, he aimed to mete out to the offender such justice as would be most fitting. If any of the outlaws' captives claimed to have no money, yet when searched were found to possess it, then, because of the lie, they were made to hand over a double gift.

"Help the good folk, and those who find life difficult," said Robin to his band; "but treat those who make it difficult as our enemies—with the Sheriff of Nottingham as the chief!"

CHAPTER 8

ASSAULT BY NIGHT

ROBIN longed to see Maid Marian once again. He knew that she was staying at Gamwell Hall now, as the guest of Squire Gamwell. Word had come to Robin that, not many days after he had gone away from Gamwell Hall with his mother, a party of the Sheriff's men had come to the Hall and charged Squire Gamwell with having shot one of the King's deer.

There had been a great battle between the Sheriff's men and the servants of Squire Gamwell. The guests that were staying at the Hall also joined in. Amongst them was Maid Marian's father.

At the height of the battle, Marian's father went to an open window and shot at the Sheriff's men. He killed many of the men with his fine shooting, but he was at last shot himself. He was taken into an inner room, and, a little later, he died.

Squire Gamwell felt very sorry for the little Maid Marian, and he told her that she could stay at Gamwell Hall with him for as long as she wished.

So Robin set out with Little John for Gamwell Hall, to see once more his childhood friend. Squire Gamwell was delighted to see Robin again. Robin introduced Little John to the Squire, and the two became friends at once. Robin's cousin, Will Gamwell, was glad that his old friend had returned. They talked for a long time. Robin told Will all that had happened since he left the Hall, and he added that if ever Will wanted to join his band he could offer him a life of freedom and excitement.

Robin, Will Gamwell, and Little John were walking through the Hall with Maid Marian, laughing and joking about old times, when Squire Gamwell burst in upon them with a very worried face.

"We are surrounded!" he said. "The Sheriff's men must have found out about your coming here."

Robin rushed at once to the window and peered into the forest, beyond the grounds of the Hall. He saw the Sheriff's men hiding in the undergrowth. There were many of them; they were well armed, and it was clear that they were in deadly earnest.

"This may be the end of everything!" said Squire Gamwell.

Robin and Little John laughed.

"It's just the sort of thing that makes life worth living," said Little John.

A tall, broad-shouldered member of the Sheriff's company bent his bow and shot an arrow towards the Hall.

"The fight has begun!" said Robin.

It was now getting dark, and little could be gained by either side. Robin knew that the next day would bring with it the full force of the battle. He knew, also, that he could take advantage of the blackness of the night to defeat the Sheriff.

He quickly worked out a plan that could be put into force at once.

"We'll show them that we are not afraid," he cried. "Who will swim the moat with me and surprise these varlets?"

Robin never asked anyone to do what he himself would not do.

Little John quickly joined him.

In those days all the largest halls had moats around them as a protection against attack. The Sheriff's men had drawn themselves together in the forest as night fell, feeling sure that nothing would happen until the light of day.

Will Gamwell followed Little John and joined Robin. Finally, two of Squire Gamwell's servants also volunteered to help.

It was an easy matter for Robin and his four friends to swim the moat and to clamber on to the bank without being seen.

As they reached the encampment where the Sheriff's men were resting, Robin very quickly told the others what he meant to do. It needed brave men to pounce upon those sleeping soldiers, for, once awakened, there would be little chance of escape for the attackers. But Robin stepped fearlessly forward. With the other men close behind him, he charged into the sleeping men, and swords flashed left and right.

The Sheriff's men were soon awake. They sprang up at once. They could not understand what was happening, for it was quite dark, and there was a scene of complete confusion. In the blackness of the night, the Sheriff's men attacked each other, not knowing who was who. Everyone was fighting with whatever weapon he could lay his hands on, and in the mêlée that followed Robin and his four gallant friends withdrew and made again for the moat.

Four of them were able to escape into the water and to swim safely to the Hall. But the fifth, one of the servants who had volunteered to join Robin, was slower than the rest, and he was caught by two of the Sheriff's men.

Robin at once started to go back to the rescue of the servant, but Squire Gamwell, when he knew what had happened, would not hear of it. He wanted the servant rescued, but it was very doubtful whether the Sheriff's men could do anything with their captive until daylight.

"Wait till morning," he said.

Robin arranged that all the men should take it in turns to keep watch from the Hall all through the night, so that any move on the part of the Sheriff and his men could be spotted. Then he ordered all the other members who were not acting as sentries to go to sleep. He wanted them to be fresh for the battle on the following day.

Maid Marian was the first to rise. She called the others as soon as day broke.

"Come!" she called to Robin. "See from this window what the men are doing with our servant."

Robin sprang to the window, and saw that the servant was about to be hanged by the Sheriff's men.

There was no time to be lost. He ordered the defenders of the Hall to finish the meal that they were eating and make ready for an attack.

He went to the window again. One of the men had climbed a tree. He carried over his shoulder a length of rope. This he tied to a bough of the tree. Underneath the bough stood a second man with the servant, who was awaiting his end without fear.

Robin called to Will Gamwell.

"Shoot the man in the tree!" he said. "And, whatever happens, do not miss!"

Will Gamwell aimed his bow carefully. Just as the arrow was winged to the target, Robin shot at the man on the ground. Both of the Sheriff's men fell. The man in the tree came tumbling through the branches and lay still on the ground.

The servant was now free, and he lost no time in running towards the moat. In he plunged and swam desperately for the Hall. Friendly hands pulled him safely out of the water when he reached the other side.

The Sheriff's men had had enough. They knew that only a long siege would now make Robin and the defenders of Gamwell Hall give in. So they withdrew, for they had not come prepared for a prolonged conflict.

They returned to the Sheriff's castle and told him of what had taken place. He was furious when he learned of their failure.

"Robin Hood must be taken!" he stormed. "If you simpletons cannot take him, I shall do so with my own hands."

Not many days were to pass before the Sheriff had that chance.

CHAPTER 9

ROBIN HOOD—BUTCHER

THE SHERIFF'S men whispered around the town that the Sheriff had himself declared he would take Robin Hood singlehanded. The news spread from mouth to mouth, and it was not long before it reached the ears of Robin Hood, who was still at Gamwell Hall.

"I'll keep the Sheriff to his word," said Robin to Marian, as they sat beneath the branches of a tall oak-tree. "If he wants to see me, I shall make certain that he does!"

Marian was concerned about Robin's intentions, for she loved him.

"Please do nothing rash," she begged. "There is no need for you to go out and look for trouble."

Robin laughed merrily. "I cannot let such an invitation pass," he said.

That same day he made preparations to leave Gamwell Hall.

"I shall be back soon. Little John will look after you." With a gay wave of his hand he was off.

"He must come back," sighed Maid Marian, watching him striding away towards the greenwood. Robin was always so brave and reckless.

Once again on his own, Robin strolled along the dusty road. Before long he met a butcher from the village, who was hurrying to the market in Nottingham to sell his meat.

An imp of mischief came into Robin's mind when he saw the butcher. He hailed the man.

"You have a fine load of meat in your cart, friend," he said. "Where are you going?"

"To Nottingham," replied the man. "It is a journey I would rather not take; but I must sell my meat to live."

"Then sell it to me," suggested Robin. "I'll buy the lot. In fact, I'll buy your horse and cart as well."

"How much will you give?" queried the butcher, cautiously.

"Whatever you want," said Robin.

The outlaw paid him a good price for his entire stock, and he paid extra for the man's old clothes. He put on the clothes and gave the butcher his own.

"Mind people don't mistake you for one of Robin Hood's band!" laughed the outlaw.

But the man could see nothing except the great bag of money in his hand. Robin had made him a rich man.

The disguised outlaw drove the cart on towards Nottingham. It was a long journey, but Robin was lighthearted and was looking forward to his visit. At last he reached the market-place in the city. There were many butchers already selling their meat. Robin watched them for a few moments to see how they offered their wares.

He set up his stand and called out to the townsfolk.

"Buy, buy, buy!" he shouted. "Big bits of beef! Lovely loins of lamb! A penny a pig!"

If Robin had no idea of prices, he had plenty of talk to help him out. With a large, dangerous-looking knife, he hacked his way through the meat and dug out great chunks. He offered them to his customers on the end of his knife—at a penny a time.

The crowd flocked about him, eager to buy his meat at the price. They were very friendly to this new butcher. Not so the other tradesmen. This stranger was ruining their trade. They were furious.

"He must be silly in the head," stormed one of the butchers. "No normal man could get a living from such prices."

"He's mad, all right," agreed another. "But that doesn't stop him from spoiling our trade."

They were glad when the Sheriff of Nottingham happened to ride into the market. That official had seen the great crowd gathered round the new butcher's stall, and he strode forward to find out what all the noise was about. He soon learned that this butcher was all but giving his meat away.

The Sheriff walked over to the man, who was now hacking again at another carcase of meat.

"Who are you?" demanded the Sheriff, as the crowd made way for him to pass.

"I'm just a poor farmer, sir," replied Robin, pretending to be as stupid as the townspeople thought him to be. "I have lands a long way from here, but my cattle bring me in little money. I thought I would sell my meat cheap to make a little extra profit."

The Sheriff laughed to himself. What a stupid man this butcher must be to think that by selling the meat cheap he would be making more profit.

"Tell me, my man," commanded the Sheriff, "how many head of cattle have you?"

"Oh, I don't know," said Robin. "I've never counted them. But there are lots of them. Well over a hundred, I should say."

Perhaps this lunatic would let the Sheriff have his cattle at a ridiculous price! It was worth trying, anyway.

"Why not sell me your beasts?" suggested the Sheriff. "You will make a great profit then."

Robin's eyes twinkled.

"You are a generous man, sire," he said in mock gratitude. "You may come with me to see my beasts whenever you wish."

The Sheriff invited Robin to eat with him at his castle, where the deal could be settled. The outlaw was laughing to himself as he went away with his foe.

"I haven't had a meal like that for a long time," said he, after the two had dined.

This was true, for the Sheriff, in his meanness, had set before Robin a very meagre meal.

"And now to business," urged the Sheriff.

The high price that Robin asked for his beasts was soon knocked down by the Sheriff. But the outlaw didn't worry what price was finally decided upon. The final figure of three hundred pounds for the entire herd seemed satisfactory to both men.

The next morning the two set off, the Sheriff on horseback and Robin in his butcher's cart.

As they came near to Sherwood Forest, the simple butcher began to talk about Robin Hood. The Sheriff was by no means a brave man, and he was a trifle nervous at the thought of meeting Robin Hood. But he did not want the butcher to notice this.

"It would give me great pleasure to meet this Robin Hood," he said boastfully. "But the scoundrel always keeps well out of my way."

"Perhaps he has heard that you are going to tackle him singlehanded," suggested the butcher.

"When I do," said the Sheriff, "I'll make him sorry he ever crossed my path."

Passing into the forest, they came upon a herd of deer.

"There," said the butcher, "that is the herd of beasts I spoke about."

The Sheriff stopped his horse.

"But these are the King's deer!" he cried angrily.

"Let me explain," laughed the butcher. He snatched his horn from under his butcher's apron and blew three loud blasts upon it. From out of the greenwood came running his Merrie Men.

"You have been so eager to meet Robin Hood in person," said the outlaw, "that I couldn't bear you to be disappointed. Here I am, at your service."

He gave a low bow. The Sheriff was frightened, and pretended to laugh off the situation.

"I'm pleased to meet you," he said. "And now that you have had your little joke, perhaps you will allow me to return to my castle."

"No, no!" replied Robin, merrily. "I am hungry and I am certain that you could eat as much as I. It would not be good manners to let you go without giving you some food, especially as the meal is so close at hand."

Robin told four men to blindfold the Sheriff. The unhappy man did not struggle. He knew he was completely in Robin's hands. Then he was led some distance into the forest to where the rest of the outlaws were preparing a meal.

The bandage was taken from the Sheriff's eyes.

"Let us make a very special feast," said the outlaw leader, to those who were preparing the meal. "We have such an important guest with us. We must honour him."

In a short while a fine feast was ready. The Sheriff was hungry after his morning ride in the cool air, and he ate heartily. He quite ignored the fact that he was eating the King's deer. Robin could not help laughing.

"We shall not tell the King that you are eating his deer," said he; "that is, of course, so long as you don't tell him yourself."

There was little that the Sheriff could say to this. He remained silent. His only wish was to get away from Robin Hood and from the forest. Robin guessed his thoughts.

"Before we part," said the outlaw, "we have a little business to attend to. Perhaps you would like to pay me now for the beasts, as we arranged last night."

"But you tricked me," shouted the Sheriff. "We were talking of cattle."

"Not at all," smiled Robin. "At no time did I mention cattle. If you recall our talks you'll remember that I referred to them always as beasts. And beasts they are."

Robin ordered his men to search the Sheriff. They soon found the bags containing the three hundred pounds in gold. These Robin Hood took.

The Sheriff's eyes were bandaged again, and he was led to the outskirts of the forest once more. Here he was set free. He returned to Nottingham a sad and angry man.

"I'll catch Robin Hood if it is the last thing I do!" he vowed as he entered his castle.

CHAPTER 10

WILL SCARLET

"IT's a wonderful morning!"

Robin prodded Little John in the ribs as he spoke. The giant was still asleep under the greenwood tree. He opened his eyes as he heard Robin's voice, and, stretching his great limbs, he rose to his feet.

"You're up early," he said to Robin. The sun was only just creeping up over the horizon, but already it was sending warm beams of yellow through the gently swaying branches overhead.

Robin set out alone into the forest, where the graceful greenery of the overhanging boughs, with the sun's first rays shining down on the leafy carpet, touched his face like friendly fingers. He longed to see Maid Marian again, and to hear her merry laughter. He loved the comradeship of his Merrie Men; but he never forgot the friendship of his earlier days. It was this longing for old faces that had set him wandering, on this particular morning, alone along the forest paths.

He had reached the edge of the forest along the Nottingham road when, suddenly, he caught sight of a young man who evidently belonged to some good family. His doublet was all of silk; his stockings were bright scarlet.

"What a bright contrast he makes to the soft greens and browns of the woodland," thought Robin. "And what a target he'd make if anyone were chasing him!"

Then Robin stopped dead in his tracks.

"Hello!" he murmured to himself. "This fellow is up to something."

The man in scarlet was standing still, his eyes fixed on a herd of deer that, unaware of his presence, were grazing some distance away.

The young man spoke. His voice was soft and cultured.

"I'll have the best of you for my meal today, and very quickly, too!"

"Heavens!" exclaimed Robin, under his breath, as he watched the young man fit an arrow to his bow and take steady aim.

Everyone knew that it was a very serious crime to kill the King's deer. The outlaws had been doing it for a long time, but this respectable young man was not an outlaw.

Robin stood silent as he saw the man pull back the arrow in the bow. The archer was almost forty yards away from the nearest wanderer from the herd, but, in spite of the distance, his arrow sped straight to its mark, and the stricken deer dropped where it stood, shot through the heart, while the rest of the animals scampered away in a panic.

"Well done! Well hit!" cried Robin loudly.

The young man in the scarlet stockings jumped in surprise. He was startled at the voice so near him. He thought at first that Robin must be one of the foresters of the place. If that were so, he knew that he had been caught red-handed in a crime sufficient to hang him. He had no wish to feel the noose around his neck. It would be better, he thought, to be the attacking party than to be the party attacked.

He acted at once.

"A second shot can be as good as the first," he cried as he took a step towards Robin, fitting a second arrow to his bow. "If you don't clear off, this will find a target in your ribs."

Robin did not move. Though the other was covering him menacingly with his bow-and-arrow, the outlaw remained fearlessly watching him. There stood the two men, facing each other. Both were unafraid; and each was waiting for the other to make a move.

Robin's face broke into a smile.

"I say again," he laughed, "well done! To bring down a deer at forty yards is the feat of a true marksman."

Suddenly the other man dropped his bow and made towards Robin with clenched fists, exclaiming: "If you don't take your carcase out of the way, I'll make you sorry that you ever saw me! What has it to do with you if I kill a deer? Answer me that!"

Robin grinned at the stranger's wrath.

"If you are so put out with a man who does nothing but pay you a compliment, what kind of a wild beast would you be to one who insulted you?"

"Drop your banter and fight me!" exclaimed the other.

"I'm willing enough to fight," returned Robin. "I love fighting for its own sake; but why should I fight you? I don't waste my time on every ill-mannered varlet who crosses my path. When I fight it is with someone of much finer mettle than you!"

Robin's tone was not bitter. It was gently sarcastic. He knew well that his mockery would not help to bring about peace.

"Boasts, mere boasts!" fumed the other.

He rushed to his bow once more to finish the argument and to avenge the insults. But, as he turned, he found that he was already covered by Robin, who had drawn his bow more quickly.

"Now," cried Robin, the smile that had been playing about his lips vanishing, "move but one step and I send this arrow flying towards you! If you want a fight, you have a sword by your side. So have I. You are obviously the son of a good family and are entitled to wear a sword. Unsheathe your blade, then, and I'll cross swords with you!"

The young man wanted no further prompting. He drew his blade immediately and there followed a clashing of steel as sword met sword.

They had not been fighting long before Robin realised that his opponent was no mean fighter. This man was a fine swordsman and Robin had hard work to hold his own. Practised as he was in every feint and pass and thrust, Robin discovered that the young man was ready for him and that he must fence with all the tricks and skill he possessed, or his own defence would be broken through.

"This is just the man for my band," said Robin to himself as they fought on, breathlessly. "A brave fellow, and skilled with his bow as well as with his sword. He's the very man for me. But, first, I must win this contest."

He pressed the stranger hard, and the other replied with fresh zeal. The clash of shining steel rang out through the forest as the two fought desperately. First Robin would drive his opponent back; then, under a renewed onslaught, he would give ground before a series of fierce thrusts.

It was not long, however, before Robin could see that his opponent was losing strength. The outlaw knew that by attacking even more fiercely, the stranger would be compelled to give in. Robin closed in with renewed energy. He flashed around the young man, bringing into play all his skill and daring. It was too much for his brave opponent. Slowly he gave way. He was being worn down.

With one terrific stroke, Robin crashed the other's sword from his hand. The stranger was completely at his mercy—and he knew it! But Robin had no wish to harm him. Instead, he dropped his own sword.

"Listen to me!" said he. "You are a tough lad, whoever you are. You should have a mind for a life of adventure."

"That's why I am here," exclaimed the other, recovering his breath. "I set out to join the band of Robin Hood."

"Oh! Did you?" smiled Robin.

It was going to be easy to persuade this young man to join him, after all!

"But why should you want to join him?" bantered

Robin. "Don't you know that every man's hand is turned against him? He is an outlaw, you know!"

"I do know. And my hand isn't turned against him, for one!" was the reply. "Tales of his adventures have spread far and wide. People who know him have described him to me. He—why, now I come to think of it, he is something like you to look at!"

"I am he!" said Robin.

"You!" The other was nonplussed, not knowing what to say.

Robin dropped his sword into its sheath. "It's strange that we should meet in this way. I must take you to my men. They will be pleased to see you. But, tell me, why did you leave your home? What have you done?"

"Well, to tell you the truth," explained the other, "I had an accident, in which I nearly killed one of my father's servants. It is not yet known whether the man will live or die."

"Hm!" mused Robin. "That may be serious."

"Yes, that's just the trouble. If he lives, everything will be all right. If he dies, you know what will happen to me if I am caught."

"You'll be dangling on the end of a rope."

"I thought the only thing to do," went on the stranger, "was to join you in the life I have heard about ever since you fled from the Sheriff of Nottingham. I ran away while I was still free and came straight here."

"Good," said the outlaw leader. "If you like adventure, we shall not disappoint you. I'll lead you to my men, and they will treat you as one of themselves."

His eyes twinkled as he spoke. It was a custom with his men to re-christen all new members. Robin had already thought of a new name for this man.

The two had been walking for some distance when they came to a glade. Here Robin blew the well-known call on his horn. Soon, men came running through the forest to him. They stopped short when they saw the strong young stranger in scarlet stockings.

"Men," called Robin, as his band eyed the newcomer, "I want you to meet a new member. He has come to join our band and to be one of us. Make him welcome—and see that he is well fed."

The men made him welcome for Robin's sake. They gave him some of their own meal and made a special feast of it in his honour.

"Now for the christening!" announced Much-the-Miller's son, when the meal was over.

"What are we to call him?" asked Will-the-Wrestler.

The outlaws were silent for a moment. Then: "What name are you known by?" asked Little John.

"I was christened—that is, first christened—William," said the youth, eyeing the preparations for his second christening curiously.

"But we cannct call him William," said Little John, "for sometimes that's what we call Will-the-Wrestler."

The outlaws suggested various names, but none could think of a suitable name for the stranger. Robin helped them out of the difficulty.

"Look at his stockings!" he laughed. "Finer scarlet never graced a young man's leg. He shall be called Will Scarlet."

The christening ceremony was carried out in front of the trestle-tables. Will Scarlet was made a member of Robin Hood's band—a valuable member, who became one of Robin's right-hand men.

CHAPTER 11

ROBIN AND THE POOR KNIGHT

INTO Sherwood Forest rode a tall knight. He was on a fine black horse that was well cared for, but looked ragged and shabby.

He was on his way to an abbey near Nottingham. It was a visit that he would have liked to avoid, for he owed the Abbot a great amount of money and he was quite unable to pay his debt. But he was an honest man, and he was going to confess that he could not pay.

Little John, bursting through the trees at the sound of the horse's hooves, hailed the knight and brought him to a stop.

"Welcome, Sir Knight!" called Little John.

Knights were fine sport for Robin and his men, for they were sometimes rich and cruel, and Robin often took some of their wealth from them to give to the poor. Little John was not to know that Sir

Richard of Lea, who now stood before him, was neither rich nor cruel.

"Will you come and dine with us?" went on Little John. "Our master will be pleased to meet you!"

"Who is your master?" asked Sir Richard.

"He is Robin Hood!" was the reply.

"I have heard a lot about him," said the knight. "I shall be pleased to meet him."

Little John took the reins of the horse in his hand and led the knight through the forest to Robin's greenwood camp. Robin came forward to meet them as the two approached. Sir Richard of Lea dismounted from his horse as Robin came up to him.

Robin saw at once the poor state that the knight was in. He looked at his worn clothes, at the shabby saddle on the horse's back, at the knight's sad expression.

"What ails you, Sir Knight?" asked he.

"Nothing ails me!" said the knight proudly, not wishing to betray his troubles to a stranger.

"Then at least accept a meal from us," said Robin.

He was puzzled by this knight. Usually wellmounted travellers had money that could be taken for the poor.

A meal was prepared. But when the knight saw such a great feast set before him he turned to Robin.

"I cannot eat," he said.

"Oh, come!" cried Robin. "You look to me as if that's just what you could do!"

"You are right," sighed the knight. "But, you see, I could not possibly pay for such a meal as you have set before me. I wouldn't eat anything for which I could not pay."

Robin Hood glanced at Little John and winked. He had heard that tale before!

"Tell me the truth," said Robin. "How much money have you with you?"

"I have no more than ten shillings," replied Sir Richard of Lea.

"Then," said the outlaw, "the meal shall not cost you anything. Sit down and eat."

When the feast was begun, Robin told Little John to search the bags that were on the knight's horse and to make sure that the knight had spoken the truth about the amount of money he carried. Little John came back after his search and told his master that there were indeed only ten shillings in the knight's moneybags.

"Tell me, good sir," said Robin, turning to Sir Richard, "how is it that you are in this sorry state?"

"'Tis a long story," replied Sir Richard, and, between mouthfuls of delicious venison, he told Robin his story. "I was once a rich man, but two years ago many of my herds died, much of my wealth was stolen, and, to crown it all, my son pierced a knight's helmet by accident in a tournament. It was decreed, after the knight had died, that my son should pay a very heavy fine. To save him from prison, I had to borrow the money from an abbot."

"An abbot, of all people!" laughed Robin.

"I promised him," Sir Richard went on, "that if I did not pay it back before a certain day I would hand over to him all my lands. That day is tomorrow. I cannot pay, and I am going to the Abbot to hand over my lands."

"But why can't you borrow the money?" asked Robin, after a pause.

The knight looked straight at his host.

"Who would lend it to a broken-down knight, when the reason he needs it is to pay off a debt?" he asked.

Robin was silent for a moment.

"I believe your story," he said, at last. "It is a misfortune that might have come to anybody. You must go to the Abbot tomorrow and beg him to give you more time to pay."

"The Abbot is a hard man, Robin Hood," said Sir Richard. "He will merely laugh in my face."

"Then you will laugh right back in his!" said Robin. "If he refuses you any more time, you must pay him the money in full. I should love to see his face change colour at that!"

"Very amusing!" said Sir Richard, sarcastically. "A good joke! But I tell you I haven't the money."

"I will lend it to you," was Robin's answer. "I trust you to pay it back to me when you can." He turned to Little John. "Go to our treasure-chest and bring to me—er—how much, Sir Richard?"

"Four hundred pounds!" said the knight.

"Bring me," went on Robin to Little John, "four hundred pounds and have it placed in a bag."

The knight was overcome with gratitude.

Before long he was seated again on his horse. Robin had asked his men to put a new saddle and bridle on the horse, while the knight was given new clothes and had his shield and helmet brightly polished.

Sir Richard was a happy man as he trotted away through the greenwood that sunny afternoon.

CHAPTER 12

TRICKING THE ABBOT

"TODAY's the day!" sang the Abbot to himself as he dressed himself with extra care. "By twelve o'clock I shall be a rich man. I'll have lands here, lands there, lands everywhere!"

He skipped as well as his portly bearing would allow to his breakfast-room. This was the day when Sir Richard of Lea was due to pay back the debt he owed. The cunning Abbot had learned that the knight was in no position to pay.

The lands that would fall into his hands were far more useful to him than the money. And today they would be his!

There came a knock on his door. A servant entered.

"The magistrate, sire," mumbled the servant.

"Show him in! Show him in!" beamed the Abbot, as he attacked his breakfast with relish. Then, as the magistrate was ushered into his presence, "Good morning! Good morning! Do sit down. Have you breakfasted?"

"Well, as a matter of fact, I have," said the magistrate. "But since you—er——"

"Why, certainly! Do join me!"

He had asked the magistrate to attend that morning so that he could watch the handing-over of Sir

c

Richard's lands. After the meal the two strolled into the grounds of the Abbey. The creeping shadow of the sundial clock showed them that the time was drawing near when Sir Richard was due to pay the money.

"It doesn't look as if your guest is going to arrive, my lord Abbot," said the magistrate.

"That will be too bad for him," said the Abbot.

"Perhaps his horse has had a fall," suggested the magistrate; "or, worse still, perhaps he has fallen into the hands of Robin Hood."

"That is not my fault," snorted the Abbot. "He can make no excuses. The agreement between the knight and myself was that the money should be paid by noon today. If it is not here by that time then his lands will be mine."

The two waited impatiently for the time to pass. The Abbot gave up trying to make conversation. He was too excited to talk. The magistrate was only concerned with seeing that justice would be done at the appointed hour. They walked round the grounds in silence.

The Abbot turned quickly when he heard the running footsteps of a monk behind him.

"There is a man on horseback in the distance, Sir Abbot!" he exclaimed.

"What!" almost screamed the Abbot. "What did he look like?"

"He was too far away for me to see," answered the monk.

The Abbot rushed into the Abbey and came out to look from the turret at the figure far away along the road. It was a knight. The Abbot could see that, for the sun glinted on the rider's helmet and shield.

He knew instinctively that it was Sir Richard. He consoled himself with the knowledge that, according to reports, the knight was in no position to pay his debts.

Presently Sir Richard rode up to the Abbey door and knocked. He was admitted to the Abbey, and he walked straight to where the Abbot and the magistrate had seated themselves.

The Abbot was quick to get down to business.

"There is little time left, Sir Richard, for the settling of your debts," he said. "Have you brought the money with you?"

He asked the question confidently, for he could see that the knight's hands were empty.

"My lord Abbot," said Sir Richard, respectfully, "I thought perhaps you would agree to take part of my debt and to grant me another year to pay the remainder."

Sir Richard laughed to himself as he spoke. The Abbot's face was almost comical in its look of sudden relief.

"Ha!" grated the Abbot. "I thought as much. I am not here to parley with you. I will have all your debt or all your lands!"

"I understand, Sir Richard," the magistrate put in, "that your agreement was to pay the debt in full today or to hand over your lands as payment."

"That is true," said Sir Richard, adopting an air of sadness. "Then, in the meantime, my lord Abbot, will you give me your blessing?" And Sir Richard knelt down to receive the Abbot's blessing.

"How dare you, sir!" stormed the Abbot. "Come, Sir Knight, we will not waste any more time. We are not here to listen to your excuses. You must pay your debt in money now, or I will have your lands. The magistrate here shall see that everything is done in order."

The Abbot did not want the money to be paid, and Sir Richard's next action stunned him as thoroughly as if he had been struck with a quarter-staff. Sir Richard pulled from behind him a great bag of money. It had been hidden there by his cloak.

The Abbot stared blankly. He tried to pull himself together. Was it possible, he asked himself, that Sir Richard could pay fully? He grabbed the bag and slowly counted the money.

"I'm glad that the magistrate is here," said Sir Richard. "He can witness that the correct amount of money has been paid."

The magistrate nodded. He looked on while the Abbot counted all the coins. The amount was correct. The Abbot was dumbfounded.

"Now perhaps you will hand over the deed that I signed, my lord Abbot," said Sir Richard, with a bow.

"You varlet!" stormed the Abbot. "You distinctly said that you were——"

"Excuse me, my lord Abbot," put in the magistrate, "you have no option but to hand over the deed, for Sir Richard has indeed paid his debt in full."

"This is outrageous!" fumed the Abbot.

He had no option, however, but to hand over the deed.

He was still speechless as Sir Richard walked out of the door, mounted his horse, and rode away from the Abbey. The knight could not help laughing at the sad figure of the Abbot as he realised that the lands he hoped for were not to be his.

Sir Richard made up his mind that directly he had enough money to repay Robin Hood he would take him the sum, with whatever else he could afford.

CHAPTER 13

THE AMBUSHED ABBOT

THE ABBOT was a sadder man when he had received the money from Sir Richard of Lea. He wondered how it was that the knight could have come safely through Sherwood Forest without being robbed by the outlaw Robin Hood. But it showed that it was at least safe to pass through the forest. He made up his mind to travel himself with the money into Nottingham and to trade it at a profit.

He gathered together all the money he kept in the Abbey. This, with Sir Richard's payment, he placed in a large bag, and set out for Nottingham. He was not a brave man, and he ordered forty-nine of his men, well armed with bows and arrows, to go with him just in case he should fall foul of Robin Hood.

He had not gone far when he realised it was unwise to place all the money in one bag. He dismounted, and, leaving only twenty coins in his bag, hid the remainder of the money in the packs that his armed men carried.

Remounting his horse, he entered the Forest of Sherwood. All was quiet and peaceful. The birds were singing gaily in the trees, and the Abbot felt brave with his forty-nine men around him.

"Halt!" cried a voice.

The Abbot stopped. He looked round, but he could see nobody. Then an arrow buried itself into the bundle of cloth upon which he was sitting. He went as white as a sheet. All the men with him waited for his words of command. None came. The Abbot was too frightened to think about fighting.

"Drop your bows, or you are all dead men!" came the voice again.

"Yes, yes, drop your bows, my men!" cried the Abbot in alarm. The worried man looked wildly about him, but the outlaws could not be seen. Though they would rather have fought, the Abbot's men could do nothing but obey their leader.

Out of the greenwood came Little John and Will Scarlet, followed by one hundred and fifty of Robin's men, with bows ready for action.

Little John walked up to the Abbot.

"Lord Abbot," he said, "our leader, Robin Hood, has sent us to invite you to join us in a merry meal. He heard that you were travelling to Nottingham on business, and he wondered whether he could satisfy your hunger and quench your thirst on the way."

The Abbot was very frightened. He called his men to follow, and the whole company trooped towards Robin's camp.

An hour later they were all gathered round the festive table in the greenwood. A great feast had been prepared, and Robin welcomed the Abbot as if he were his best friend. When the meal was finished, Robin turned to him.

"It is the custom for my guests to pay something towards the meals they have with us," he said. "If he is a poor man he gets it for nothing. But if he is a rich man he pays heavily both for the meal he has had and for those before him who had theirs free. So tell me, my lord Abbot, what you are inclined to pay for yourself and your men."

The Abbot spoke as bravely as he could.

"You can see," he said, "that we are travelling to Nottingham. I take little money with me, for a man in my position has no business with large sums of money. Indeed, I have only twenty coins on me. I am sure you could not take those from us, for they must last us until my return."

"If that is the truth," replied Robin, "you shall have your meal free. But is it the truth?"

The Abbot declared that he had told the truth, and Robin seemed to be satisfied with his answer. But suddenly he turned to the Abbot.

"My lord Abbot," he said, "while you have been feasting, my men have searched the packs of your horses, and it was as if we walked into a treasury. You have tried to deceive me. If you had told the truth I would have scorned to lay hands on the money of trustful men. As it is, you must pay for your men —there are forty-nine of them, with big appetites— and for yourself, with the biggest appetite of them all. I shall charge you five pounds apiece for the meal, and we shall be glad to see you again some other day. There will also be a fine of a hundred and fifty pounds because you tried to deceive me. Strangely enough, the total sum is the same as the amount that a certain Sir Richard of Lea paid to you as a debt."

The Abbot was amazed. He could understand now how Sir Richard had been able to pay his money. But it was useless to protest. He paid the price and went off, a sadder man.

Some months later, when Sir Richard of Lea had retrieved his fortunes, he set out to pay back the money he had borrowed from Robin.

But Robin told him that the debt was already paid, for the Abbot had returned the money on his way to Nottingham!

CHAPTER 14

FRIAR TUCK

ONE DAY Robin sat down by the side of a cool forest stream. He had not been there long when he heard the voices of two men, who appeared to be arguing.

"One of the best streams in the country," said one voice.

"Ridiculous!" argued the other. "There's not a fish to be seen in the whole stream."

The voices were getting nearer to where Robin sat, and, as they became louder, he thought how strangely alike they were. He listened intently, and the argument went on. Neither of the voices seemed to be getting annoyed, though each had very different opinions about the merits of the stream.

A very fat man came into view through the trees on the opposite side of the stream. Robin could see that he was a friar by the clothes he wore. His head was almost bald—just a narrow fringe of hair circled his shiny head. The strange thing was that he was alone.

Robin looked round for a second man, but he could see no one.

"It's useless to fish in this stream," said the friar.

Then he answered himself: "Take me to a better stream, if you can!"

So that was it. The friar was arguing with himself! Robin watched silently as the friar made ready to fish. He was still arguing with himself when Robin's voice interrupted him.

"Good morning!" called the outlaw. "How are you both?"

"Oh, we're fine!" returned the friar.

"I want to cross the stream," stated Robin.

"Then cross it!" replied the friar, flatly.

"How can I?" questioned the outlaw.

"In the same way as I would. You'll have to wade across."

"I don't think that'll be necessary."

"Oh? Perhaps you can fly?" said the friar, humorously.

He turned his attention again to his fishing, as if he had dismissed the outlaw from his mind. But only for a moment.

"My friend!" called Robin, sternly.

The friar looked up suddenly, to see himself covered by Robin's bow. The friar was not alarmed. He looked at the outlaw calmly.

"Carry me across this stream!" ordered Robin.

"Is that the way you usually ask a favour?" inquired the friar. "If you wanted me to carry you across, why didn't you ask me before?"

He stood up, and, leaving his sword on the bank, he slipped into the stream and waded across to where Robin stood.   As he reached the bank he said: "Climb on my back.   And the next time you ask to be taken across the stream, try to be more civil."

Robin climbed on the friar's broad back, and the fat fellow waded slowly back across the stream.   It was dangerous walking on the stony bed.   The friar slipped, but managed to right himself.   The two reached the opposite bank in safety.

The friar shook himself when he was on dry grass again.   Quickly he dived down for his sword and swung round upon Robin.

"Now it's my turn," he said.   "I want to cross the stream, and you are going to carry me!"

Robin was too close to the friar to use his bow.   He smiled at the fat's man's boldness.   Here was someone with courage and a sense of humour.   Robin bowed respectfully to him.

"That's fair enough," he said.   "Jump on my back—if you're not too fat."

Robin slid into the water and the wet friar clambered on his back.   The fat man was very heavy, and Robin staggered about in mid-stream with his great load.   The friar was chuckling all the time.   Robin struggled quietly on, and at last reached the opposite bank.   As the portly friar was let down on the grass, he burst into laughter.

"This is all so stupid!" he cried.   "Whatever shall we be doing next?"

"Next, my dear friar," said Robin, calmly, "you will be carrying me back again across the stream."

The friar stopped laughing. It was no longer funny!

"Well, all right, if you say so," he agreed. "But let this be the last time."

Robin climbed again on the fat man's back. They waded across the shallow water, and soon reached mid-stream. The friar's step was not quite so steady this time, and he had not gone much more than halfway before his foot tripped on a stone, and he fell forward.

Robin was pitched clean off his broad back, and went crashing into the water. As if nothing had happened, the holy man kept wading towards the bank, where he climbed out and started to shake himself dry.

"You did that purposely," shouted Robin, angrily, as he picked himself up and scrambled to the bank after the friar. "You shall pay heavily for it."

"Upon my word——" began the friar. But he did not finish the sentence, for suddenly Robin was upon him.

There was no thought of weapons. The two men fought with their fists. In spite of his fatness, the friar was very strong, and he gave Robin some hard knocks. They fought on for a few moments, when Robin, seeing how silly it all was, stopped fighting.

"You're a strong-hearted fellow," he said to the friar. "It is silly for us to fight each other. You are a man after my own heart."

The friar straightened his dripping robes as best he could.

"I try to be at peace with every man," he said, still breathing hard after the fight. "But it was you who wanted combat. Let us now shake hands."

The two shook hands and became friends. Robin told him what would have happened if he were in danger.

"Three blasts on my trusty horn would have made you think the very forest was alive," he said.

"Why, does it frighten all the animals away?" laughed the friar.

Robin put the horn to his lips. In a short while many of his Merrie Men came bounding through the forest to join him. Little John was the first to reach his side.

"Friar Tuck!" exclaimed Little John. "What brings you here?"

"Do you know him?" asked Robin, in surprise.

"Know him!" laughed Little John. "He used to be the one man who could beat me at archery. We are friends of long standing."

"And you," said Friar Tuck, turning to Robin, "must be Robin Hood, the outlaw."

"I am he," said Robin.

"What a shame!" murmured the friar, shaking his head. "To think that I should have carried on my back a man who does not respect the law of the country."

"I and my band do far more good than we do harm," asserted the outlaw. "We take from the rich to help the poor. That is what the law should do."

"I think the Sheriff of Nottingham would disagree with you," said the friar, still sadly shaking his head. "However, there's something in what you say. Poor people do need helping. Look at me, for instance!"

Robin eyed him suspiciously.

"I could help you to lose some of your fat," he said. "But show us, friar, your skill with the bow."

The friar put two fingers to his mouth and whistled loudly. A great dog came bounding towards him. It was his own animal, and he had trained it to stand perfectly still with a stone balanced on its head.

"Watch this!" said the friar.

He drew his bow, and, at a good distance, shot the arrow straight towards the dog. The stone was knocked off the animal's head. The dog was untouched.

"A perfect shot!" Robin congratulated him. "Friar Tuck, will you join my band? We need a good man and true; and we need a chaplain to help us to mend some of our wild ways."

The friar was quiet for a while. He was arguing with himself again, though he did not speak aloud this time. At length he said: "I'll join you, if you think I should be useful."

The Merrie Men cheered heartily. From that moment Friar Tuck became a member of Robin's band—and he was almost the only member to join without christening. The Merrie Men decided that his recent adventure in the stream was christening enough for him!

CHAPTER 15

VENGEANCE ON SIR GUY

"It's no good going to Gamwell Hall, Robin," said the old lady as she stopped working at her spinning-wheel to face the outlaw.

"Why not?" asked Robin, stretching himself lazily in the woman's old fireside chair.

He had visited this aged friend while he was near Nottingham, and had told her of his intention of going to Gamwell Hall.

"Because it doesn't belong to Squire Gamwell any longer," was the old lady's reply.

"Indeed?" cried Robin. "But what of Maid Marian, and Will Gamwell? I promised Maid Marian that I would return, and return I shall!"

"Squire Gamwell is dead," said the old lady, quietly. "Sir Guy of Gisborne lives in the old Hall now."

Robin could hardly believe her. It was not the knowledge that the kindly old squire had died that disturbed him; it was the news that Sir Guy of Gisborne, a knight hated by Squire Gamwell, should be in residence.

"But surely Squire Gamwell would have left the Hall to his own son?" questioned the outlaw.

"Ah, he would have done if he could."

"What do you mean?"

"It was like this, Robin," the old woman continued: "Sir Guy of Gisborne attacked Gamwell Hall in great force one day. There was a terrific battle, and it ended in the Squire being killed and the Hall taken by Sir Guy."

"What happened to Maid Marian?" was Robin's quick question.

"I don't know," replied the old woman. "Nobody knows."

"You mean to say she has vanished?" Robin was astounded.

"Some say she was away at the time of the attack. Some say Sir Guy of Gisborne held her prisoner and married her. Some say he killed her."

Robin stared blindly out through the window. Could it be true that Maid Marian—his Maid Marian —was dead? No! That could never be. He reeled out into the sunlight. Revenge against Sir Guy of Gisborne filled his mind.

When he returned to his greenwood camp, he called about him all his men.

"We are going to attack Gamwell Hall," he announced. "Sir Guy of Gisborne has captured the Hall and killed our friend, Squire Gamwell. What has become of Maid Marian and Will Gamwell nobody knows. We are going to find that out."

"What plans have you, master?" asked Little John.

"None, except that we attack tonight!"

It was dark that night. As Robin's men set out through the forest they talked excitedly amongst themselves about the daring attack they were about to make. Robin led them to the outskirts of the greenwood, across fields, and along darkened country lanes. At last the lights of Gamwell Hall could be seen in the distance.

"Quiet, men," ordered Robin. "Not a word until we have reached the Hall."

All speech ended. Only the soft tread of stealthy footsteps could be heard on the night air.

"Here's the moat," whispered the outlaw leader, as the party halted on the bank.

The cold dark water, rippling now and then as the breeze touched it, looked forbidding as some of the lights from the Hall sent shafts of yellow through it.

"Little John and Will Scarlet," breathed Robin, "I want you to swim the moat and then to creep up to the windows. Find out what is happening in the Hall and return to us. We shall cross the moat while you are gone and we'll meet you on the far side."

Little John and Will Scarlet slipped into the deep water and swam silently away from the party of men. They were not gone long. Robin's men had crossed the moat and were silently waiting on the other side of the water when the two men met them.

"Sir Guy is holding a feast," reported Little John. "They are making merry."

"That's lucky for us," said Friar Tuck. "It will be Robin Hood and his Merrie Men against Sir Guy and his Merrie Men."

"They will not be so merry when they have felt our steel," said Robin. "Now," he added softly, "advance through the fence."

Friar Tuck was the first to attempt to get through the fence. There was a hole in it, the hole that Little John and Will Scarlet had climbed through. But Friar Tuck was a man of very different proportions. His head and shoulders were through before he realised that his great girth would not allow the rest of him to follow. He was pulled back by those behind him. The fence was torn down bit by bit until a hole large enough for the men to climb through in pairs was made.

"I'm going alone to the door of the Hall," said Robin, when all the men were standing in the grounds. "Keep silent and follow me in the shadows."

Robin went on ahead. He reached the door, and knocked.

"What do you want?" asked the doorkeeper, peering through the darkness at his visitor.

"Is Sir Guy at home?" asked Robin.

"He is."

"Then tell him that Robin Hood has come to see him."

Amazement showed on the doorkeeper's face as the light from inside the Hall fell on his rugged features. He took a step backwards. Was this really Robin Hood in person?

"I—I'll tell Sir Guy," he stammered. "Are you alone?"

"Do I look as if I have anyone with me?"

Again the doorkeeper peered into the night. He could see nobody.

" Wait!" he said.

He ran into the Hall and told Sir Guy of Gisborne.

"Robin Hood, eh?" laughed Sir Guy. "Tell him to come in."

"But he cannot be up to any good, sire."

"If Robin Hood wants to put his head in a noose, let him do so," shouted the knight.

"I fear he has some trick up his sleeve."

"Admit him, I say!" cried Sir Guy, smiting the table with his fist.

The doorkeeper said no more. He went back to the entrance and opened the door again. While he had been talking to Sir Guy, the rest of Robin's men had been slowly creeping towards the leader. Now they were all standing waiting at the door.

"You may enter," said the doorkeeper. "Sir Guy will see you in the Hall."

"Then out of our way," cried Robin, thrusting the man aside.

The Merrie Men followed Robin down the Hall to where Sir Guy was feasting at a trestle-table with many knights. Around the walls were posted a number of Sir Guy's soldiers.

"Who gave leave for all those men to come in?" demanded Sir Guy. He had expected the outlaw to come alone down the Hall, and here he intended to insult him before taking him captive. But the sight of all Robin's archers made him rise up in terror.

"Villains!" he screamed. "Slay them! Let not a single man remain alive!"

"Every man for himself!" shouted Robin, and dashed for the knight.

A terrific fight followed. Sir Guy's men were in the best position, for they had swords and battle-axes. These were more suitable for close-quarter fighting. But Robin and his men were strong, fresh and determined.

The two sides charged into each other furiously. Sir Guy's soldiers were brave and strong. They were used to fighting; but Robin's men were hardy, and they had sprung a great surprise by their sudden arrival. Robin's words of encouragement rang in their ears as they sprang forward to attack. Whenever one of Sir Guy's soldiers fell, his sword was snatched by one of Robin's men. The soldiers were no match for the determined men from Sherwood Forest, and soon they were falling back before the outlaws.

Suddenly Robin Hood cried a warning. An oil-lamp he had seen swinging dangerously as a sword crashed into it suddenly fell to the floor. Another followed. Then another. The Hall was rapidly getting darker as lamp after lamp crashed to the floor.

Robin was still grappling with Sir Guy of Gisborne when the last of the lamps was hit and the Hall plunged into darkness. In that moment Sir Guy acted with great cunning. In the confusion, he slipped free of Robin and made for the door of the Hall. In the darkness it was impossible to follow him. Neither side could tell who was who.

Suddenly fire flared up. One of the oil-lamps had set light to part of the timbered wall of the Hall. The flames spread quickly. The whole building would be burning before long. Robin called his men together.

"Sir Guy has escaped," he shouted. "It's useless fighting on in this inferno. We must leave these rascals and return to the forest."

As the flames spread, Robin's men made their way out of the burning building and crossed the grounds to the moat. Some were being helped along by others. Two of the men had to be left behind. They had been killed by the soldiers.

"This is a sad sight," murmured Robin to Friar Tuck, as they stood for a moment on the other side of the moat watching the flames leaping high into

the air. "The gallant Gamwell Hall that I have loved
for so many years will soon be no more."

But Robin's mind wandered from the Hall. He
had set out to rescue the beautiful Maid Marian
from Sir Guy of Gisborne; yet he had seen no sign
of her.

"One thing is certain," he reflected. "Maid Marian
was not at the Hall tonight. Even if she were in
another part of the building she would have come to
find out the cause of the uproar."

Then he thought that perhaps the story that Sir
Guy had killed Maid Marian might be true, after all.
What of Will Gamwell, too? These were disturbing
questions.

As he wandered deeper into the forest towards
his encampment, he asked himself again and again:
"Where was Maid Marian?"

The answer to that question came some days later.

CHAPTER 16

CAPTURE AND ESCAPE

Sir Guy of Gisborne returned on the following
day to Gamwell Hall. As his horse drew near,
the knight's face suddenly went white. There was
no Hall. Only a smoking ruin stood before him, a
ghastly reminder of the cost of his fight against Robin
Hood.

"He's scored a great victory over me," fumed Sir Guy, seething with anger. "There's only one fitting revenge for this—the death of Robin Hood!"

He set off to visit the Sheriff of Nottingham. Together they should be able to work out a satisfactory plan. Sir Guy did not receive much encouragement at first from the Sheriff.

"I've been trying for so long to bring Robin Hood to the gallows," he said, "that I sometimes wonder whether the man is bewitched."

"He's no more bewitched than you or I," returned Sir Guy. "The secret is that he's got to be captured by cunning rather than by force. He is too bold and clever to be taken by a straightforward attack."

"Then what do you suggest?" queried the Sheriff, keen to try anything that would bring his foe to the scaffold.

"I'm going to disguise myself as a traveller," said the knight. "I intend to set out alone into the forest and by hook or by crook I shall find Robin Hood's camp. There I shall deal with the man in his own way."

"He has so many ways of his own," the Sheriff warned him.

"Do you not know that I am about the best swordsman in the country," Sir Guy boasted.

"I have heard it said," admitted the Sheriff.

"That is how I shall fight Robin Hood—with my sword. But I shall bring him to you alive—at the sword's point. So you can have the gallows prepared for my return."

"How shall I know you have been successful?" asked the Sheriff.

Sir Guy thought for a moment.

"I will tell you," he said. "When I have captured Robin Hood I will blow a long note on a hunting horn."

The Sheriff did not share Sir Guy's confidence. Nevertheless he agreed to the plan and promised to listen for the sound of the horn.

The knight wasted no time. He arranged for the clothes of a traveller to be brought to him, and, slinging the hunting horn round his neck, set out alone into the forest.

Robin, in his greenwood camp, had asked Will Scarlet and Little John to go into Nottingham that same morning to buy some new green cloth.

"The fight of last night has torn many of our uniforms," he said. "These must be renewed at once. Most of them were worn out even before the fight."

Little John and Will Scarlet, disguised as poor travellers, parted a short distance before reaching Nottingham, so that no suspicion would be aroused. Will Scarlet bought a large quantity of the green cloth from a merchant in the city. He regretted his action almost at once, for he could sense that the man was suspicious of this poor traveller buying such a large amount of green material. Will Scarlet left the shop and hurried away.

As he looked back, he saw the merchant running across the road.

"The Sheriff will know all about me in a very short time," Will said to himself. "Now I come to think of it, I should have bought small quantities of the stuff at different shops. However, it's too late to worry now."

The merchant did not stop running until he came

to the Sheriff's office. He told his tale almost before he had recovered his breath.

The Sheriff ordered some of his men to chase the outlaw, passing on to them the merchant's description of the man.

That was the sight that met Little John's eyes as he entered the town. Having taken a different route, he was a long way behind Will Scarlet. But as he strolled along the city road, disguised as a traveller, he gasped as he saw his friend being chased by six of the Sheriff's men.

"Great heavens!" cried Little John. "He'll never outdistance those men if he holds on to all that cloth."

Though Will Scarlet's bundle of cloth was hindering him, he was making good progress. He was very fleet of foot, and now he was running for his life. The added weight began to tire him, and before long one of his pursuers began to gain on him. Suddenly Will stopped dead.

"Ah, my good comrade is caught!" murmured Little John, wondering how to act to aid Will Scarlet.

But Will was not at the end of his resources. He dropped his bundle, put an arrow to his bow, and, turning, shot the nearest of the runners through the heart. This was quickly followed by a second arrow. Another man dropped. Will picked up his bundle of cloth and ran on again. His pursuers stopped when the second man fell.

"Good shooting!" cried Little John, happily, quite forgetting everything in the excitement of watching his escaping friend.

It was Little John's bad luck that the Sheriff should be coming down the road at that moment. He heard the outlaw's cry.

"Good shooting, eh?" he echoed. He turned to the men who were with him. "Catch that man!" he yelled, pointing to Little John. "He's one of Robin Hood's men, too, I'll swear!"

Little John ran off. It was no use seeking to put up a fight in such a crowd. He ran swiftly; but the Sheriff's men closed in on him from all directions. At last he was tripped, and fell headlong to the ground. He put up a terrific struggle, but despite his great strength his captors were too many for him.

With his hands bound tightly behind him, Little John was led up a hill. The Sheriff came up to him.

"Good shooting!" he sneered. "I'll show you what's good for you." He turned to his men. "Hang this dog," he said. "Hang him now as a proof to the people that I mean business with Robin Hood's band."

Little John laughed in the Sheriff's face. He realised that his last moment had come. He determined to face death as he had faced life. He did not flinch as the rope was made ready to be placed around his neck.

In the distance a horn was heard. It gave one long clear note. The Sheriff knew what that meant. It signified that someone even more important to him than Little John had been captured. This was indeed a black day for the outlaws!

"This is indeed a great day," he said to his men. "You heard that horn? It was a signal arranged by Sir Guy of Gisborne and myself. It means that he has captured Robin Hood.

"Now, dog," sneered the Sheriff, turning to Little John, "you and your master will hang together."

John did not move. The news that Robin was captured came as a terrible blow to him. But he did not let the Sheriff see his feelings.

"Ha!" he laughed at the Sheriff. "You couldn't hang Robin Hood even if you had a thousand men with you."

Brave words, these, but Little John's stout heart was heavy.

Sir Guy came into view. He was dragging Robin Hood along with him. The ragged outlaw looked as if he had had enough. It was a sorry sight for Little John to watch, even in his last moments.

The two men advanced to where Little John stood with the Sheriff and two hangmen.

"Good work, Sir Guy!" cried the Sheriff.

Suddenly, Sir Guy of Gisborne threw off his cloak. The Sheriff stared, his eyes goggling. It was not Sir Guy of Gisborne. It was Robin Hood himself! The man beside him was Will Scarlet.

There was no time for explanations to Little John. Robin cut through his bonds, and the three men fought their way through the crowd. The Sheriff and his men were too taken aback to act in time to prevent the escape of the three outlaws, who reached the safety of the forest in which they had their home.

They slowed down to a walk.

"But, master," cried Little John, breathlessly, "how did you manage to put over such a bold scheme? It was my blackest moment. I really thought it was the end of me—and of you."

Robin told him.

He had been walking along the Nottingham road, as he often did, when he came across an old traveller.

In the conversation, the traveller was very inquisitive and asked him many questions.

"Does Robin Hood live in these parts?"

"I believe he lives in the forest near here," was Robin's reply.

"I seek him," said the stranger.

"So do many people," the outlaw answered.

"But I shall catch him. Do you see this sword? Do you see this shining mail under my clothing? I am no traveller. Sir Guy of Gisborne is as clever as the foe he hunts."

"Wonderful!" smiled Robin, with mock admiration in his voice. "But suppose you meet Robin Hood with all his Merrie Men?"

"Ah! I have thought of that. Do you see this horn? A number of short blasts will warn the Sheriff of Nottingham that I need his help."

"And when you capture the outlaw—what then?"

"One long blast will tell the Sheriff to prepare the gallows."

"A clever scheme," said Robin. "But it's too bad of me, Sir Guy; I should have introduced myself to you before."

Sir Guy of Gisborne turned quickly. A sudden realisation came to him.

"I am Robin Hood," laughed the outlaw.

Robin told Little John of the furious fight that followed, and of its end, when Robin had thrust his sword through the knight's heart, killing him.

Will Scarlet took up the tale.

"When I escaped from the Sheriff's men," he began, "I stopped some way along the road and turned to see if I was still being followed. It was then that I saw you, Little John, being prepared for the hanging. I

ran quickly to tell Robin, and to my great relief I saw
our leader standing over the dead body of Sir Guy.
He quickly put on Sir Guy's clothes, and we came
back, as you saw, to your rescue."

The three comrades walked on into the forest.
Once again the Sheriff of Nottingham had been
foiled.

CHAPTER 17

ROBIN HOOD'S WEDDING

ALL THIS happened the day after the burning of
Gamwell Hall. Robin was still worried about the
fate of Maid Marian. He loved the girl dearly and
had thought many times of asking her to marry
him; but he knew that the life he was leading was
no life for a young lady of gentle upbringing. He
felt it would have been unfair to ask Maid Marian
to share his forest adventures.

If Robin had only known Marian's true feelings
he would have acted differently. She was in love
with Robin, just as he was with her, and would have
followed him to the ends of the earth if he had asked
her. But she believed that he preferred to live a wild
life with his men in the forest.

When Sir Guy of Gisborne attacked Gamwell
Hall, Maid Marian and Will Gamwell, Robin's boy-
hood friend, had both been away visiting relatives.
When they returned to find the Hall burned down

and Squire Gamwell killed, they realised that now they were without a home at all. What could they do?

"I shall avenge my father's death," said Will, grimly.

"How can you?" asked Maid Marian, and there was little hope in her voice.

"I shall join Robin in the forest," he declared.

"Oh, Will, that is indeed the right thing to do," said Marian eagerly. Her eyes brightened at the thought. She was silent for a moment. Then, at length, she looked up at her cousin: "Will!"

"Yes, Marian?"

"Take me with you into the forest."

"What?"

"I want to go with you. I want to—to join Robin Hood, too."

"But that is impossible. What could a girl do in the greenwood? It's a hard life, you know."

"It is no harder than living without a home."

Will did not reply. Maid Marian had lost her parents, her home, everything. Will knew that she loved Robin. Perhaps, after all, it would be the best thing of all—so long as Robin thought so, too.

"What will Robin say?" he asked the girl.

"We will surprise him," she replied, smiling.·

They said no more. They packed their few belongings and entered the forest that afternoon. It was early evening when they came into Robin Hood's camp.

"We have visitors, master!" called Much-the-Miller's son, as he saw the two figures approaching.

Robin came into the glade.

"Marian!"

The outlaw's face broke into a happy smile as he ran to meet the girl he had long wanted to see again. He was so eager to hear all that they had done since he last saw them that it was some time before Will and Marian could tell him of their decision to join the Merrie Men. Robin's face became serious when finally they were able to tell him their news; but only for a moment. His secret hope that Marian would one day join him was now realised.

"Let me show you how we live," he invited them, proudly.

He took Maid Marian and Will round the camp, pointing out to them various members of the band, and showing them how the food was prepared, where they ate, and how the Merrie Men spent their time.

Marian said that she, like Robin, could be happy in the forest. She soon settled down to life in the greenwood, and quickly endeared herself to the outlaw company. Robin Hood and she were specially happy together, and spent pleasant hours in close company in the forest.

What was more, the lost fortunes of Gamwell Hall had altered Robin's view towards marriage. Marian wanted Robin as a husband, and the two decided that they should marry and go on living in the forest together.

The wedding was fixed for an evening in spring. Robin and Marian stood under the fresh green leaves of a tall oak-tree. Above them the green-leaved branches hung gracefully down, like the tracery-roof of a cathedral. Birds sang in the boughs.

Friar Tuck stood in front of the couple, and around them were grouped in silence the Merrie Men.

Marian had made a wedding-dress for herself, and
she looked beautiful as she stood quietly on the green-
and-brown carpet of the forest by the side of her
lover. Robin's men had smartened up their clothes
of Lincoln Green for this great occasion. Little John
and Will Scarlet were in the forefront of the company.

When the marriage ceremony was over, the Merrie
Men sang a hymn lustily, their voices ringing bravely
through the greenwood. Robin kissed his bride.
Marian was now his wife. His greatest ambition had
been achieved.

Twang!

An arrow whizzed through the air and embedded
itself in the tree behind Robin and Marian. The
peaceful scene was shattered. Who had shot the
arrow?

"Whoever winged that arrow shall die!" cried
Robin. Quickly he entrusted Marian to the safety of
a group of his men. "Guard her with your lives!"
he commanded.

He ran through the greenwood. Some distance
away, he saw a strong band of the Sheriff's men.
They had crept up silently, guided by the outlaws'
voices raised in song. Robin could see them easily
now through the trees. Their bright-coloured coats
made a sharp contrast against the forest shades.

It was a desperate situation for Robin Hood and
his followers.

Only twelve of his men were armed. They could
not easily be seen amongst the trees because of their
suits of Lincoln green; but that was the only advantage they had now that the Sheriff's men had sprung
a surprise.

Robin decided at once on a bold plan. The Sheriff, unwisely, had arranged his men in one long line. This Robin noticed, and he was going to try to turn it to advantage.

"I want the twelve archers to line up, not too close to one another," he said. "Three unarmed men will stand behind each archer."

The men took up their positions quickly and silently.

"The archers shall shoot steadily. Each arrow must find a mark. As soon as any archer is tired his place shall at once be taken by one of the waiting men."

The men understood his plan, and, at his order, let their arrows fly. Thus Robin kept up a continuous barrage of arrows, and the Sheriff, not being able to see the men clearly, thought a huge force of Robin's men was hidden there.

All the outlaws were trained marksmen, and not an arrow was wasted. The Sheriff watched his soldiers falling one by one. There was nothing for it but to retire. When an arrow pierced his hat he waited no longer. He turned his horse round and galloped away. This was a signal to his men, who stopped shooting and fled.

"Shall we follow them, master?" cried Little John.

"No!" replied Robin, with a smile. "Have you forgotten, Little John, that this is my wedding day?"

CHAPTER 18

LITTLE JOHN'S TRICK

"It is high time that Robin Hood was brought to justice!"

As the Sheriff of Nottingham looked out from a window towards Sherwood Forest, the thoughts that were so often in his mind came to the surface.

Not far away, in Sherwood Forest, Robin Hood was thinking of the Sheriff of Nottingham.

"It is high time the Sheriff was made uncomfortable!" he told himself.

He strolled around his camp; but he soon dismissed the Sheriff from his mind when the inviting smells of breakfast were wafted towards him on the breeze.

The two men were forever plotting against each other. The Sheriff was eager to bring the outlaw to the gallows; Robin Hood was constantly playing tricks on him, for the outlaw knew the hatred that the Sheriff had for him and his band.

When, therefore, Little John told Robin that he had thought of a new trick to play on the Sheriff, Robin was keen to hear about it.

"What is it all about?" he asked.

"It is my own scheme, master," replied Little John. "I would rather like to try it before I tell you about it."

Robin did not press his faithful servant. He knew that Little John would tell him when necessary all about his plan. But he was surprised indeed when he awoke the following morning to be told that Little John was missing from the camp.

The giant had arisen early and made his way to the castle of Sir Richard of Lea.

"Good Sir Richard," said Little John when he was shown into the knight's room, "I have tired of life in the greenwood. I would like to join your service as one of your soldiers."

There was something in the way that Little John spoke that caused Sir Richard to doubt the genuineness of the outlaw's request. It was as if Little John had something up his sleeve. However, the good knight was pleased to have a man of such strength amongst his soldiers, and he allowed him to stay.

Little John became a popular man amongst the other guards at the castle. In less than a month he had become well known as the finest archer in Sir Richard's service.

It was not surprising, therefore, that when some sports were to be held in Nottingham Little John was the first to be chosen amongst Sir Richard's soldiers as a contestant.

"The man seems very eager to enter the shooting match," mused Sir Richard to himself. "I somehow feel that Little John has a secret reason for being in my service."

Dressed in scarlet livery, Sir Richard's archers, with Little John at their head, marched into Nottingham on the day of the sports, ready to try their skill in the shooting match. It would have horrified the townsfolk of the city if they had known that the giant

D

who was soon outclassing everybody with his marvellous feats with the bow-and-arrow was, in fact,
one of Robin Hood's outlaws.

The Sheriff of Nottingham was amazed at Little
John's skill, and he was excited when the time came
for the presentation of prizes. There was no doubt
about the winner.

"You have a fine aim," the Sheriff congratulated
him as he gave the prize to Little John. "I could
do with you in my service. How does that appeal
to you?"

"I should like it very much, sire," said Little John,
eagerly.

"What is your name?" asked the Sheriff.

"Er—Reynold Greenleaf," replied Little John. It
was the only name that came to his mind.

Arrangements were made between Sir Richard
and the Sheriff for the transfer of Little John's service
from the knight to the Sheriff. Sir Richard was
unwilling to allow his giant servant to serve under
the Sheriff, but he caught the twinkle in Little John's
eye, and guessed that this had been the outlaw's plan
from the very beginning. It was all clear to him
now, and he gave his permission for the transfer to
take place.

"I will pay you double your present wage, Reynold Greenleaf," said the Sheriff. "You will be one
of my archers—a high honour for any man. I will
clothe you and find you lodgings and food."

So Little John entered the Sheriff's service, and,
for a little while, all went well. But Little John was
only awaiting an opportunity. He would strike at
just the right moment.

He discovered that the Sheriff was a mean man to

his servants. Few of them received their wages at the proper time. Their food was poor, and Little John remembered hungrily the great feasts he had enjoyed in Sherwood Forest. How he longed to rejoin Robin Hood and his Merrie Men!

"Reynold Greenleaf!" called the Sheriff one day. "I am going to a distant town with some of my men. You shall stay in charge of my castle until I return."

"Very good, sire," said Little John.

The steward, who had been left to feed the remaining guards, was a lazy man. He troubled little about the cooking, and he didn't offer Little John anything to eat at all.

On the day after the Sheriff had left, Little John entered the kitchen and saw the steward idly sleeping in a chair.

"I haven't had a bite to eat," said he. "Food I must have, Sir Steward, and I intend to have it now."

The steward awoke suddenly.

"Eh?" he asked, rubbing his eyes.

"I want some food!" growled Little John.

"Then get it," retorted the surly steward.

Little John made a grab at the steward, who fled towards the door. The outlaw sprang after him and knocked him down. The steward did not move after that. Little John helped himself to a fine meal.

"What's been going on here?"

The demand came from the doorway. Little John glanced slowly round. Leaning against the doorpost was the burly figure of the cook.

"I felt hungry," said Little John, in a matter-of-fact tone. "The steward told me to get my own food. So I did."

"What is the steward doing on the floor?"

"Oh, he kept getting in my way," laughed Little John.

The cook took down a large staff from the wall and set about this new servant. He guessed what had happened. The greedy man had knocked out the steward and had stolen some food! Little John saw the cook grab the staff. He, too, found one, and they went for each other, giving blow for blow. After half an hour they both paused for rest.

"You're a strong fellow," said Little John; "and brave as well."

"You're not so helpless yourself!" returned the cook.

"If you can shoot as well, why not come with me and join Robin Hood and his Merrie Men?" suggested Little John.

"And who are you that you can make such an offer?" asked the cook curiously.

"Men call me Little John," was the reply.

He told the cook how he had become one of the Sheriff's archers. The cook laughed at the joke.

"I'll go with you," he decided. "The life would appeal to me. But we must go at once before the steward here wakes up."

"Yes," agreed Little John; "but we can't go empty-handed. The Sheriff owes me some wages."

"He owes me some, too," said the cook.

"Then let's pay ourselves, and charge the Sheriff interest," laughed the outlaw.

They strode to the Sheriff's private room and broke open desks and drawers. They gathered together a great bag of gold, and took all the Sheriff's silver dishes. These they crammed into two sacks.

"Robin Hood will have dinner in style today!" chuckled Little John, as the two made their way through the forest.

At length they came in sight of the outlaws' camp deep in the greenwood. The Merrie Men were seated round their camp-fires.

"Why, look who's here!" gasped Robin, springing to his feet as his old friend returned.

The two men staggered towards Robin with their loaded sacks over their shoulders.

"Hello, master!" called Little John.

"What are you doing in the Sheriff's colours?" asked Robin.

"Oh, I'm one of the Sheriff's men. At least, I was until a short time ago."

Robin laughed heartily when he had heard the whole story.

"When the Sheriff returns he will be in such a rage as to shake the city of Nottingham!" laughed the outlaw leader. "Something tells me that we shall have a visit from him before long."

Robin was right!

CHAPTER 19

TRAPPING THE SHERIFF

EARLY the next day Robin and Little John sat together over their breakfast.

"I wonder how long it will be before my joke is found out," said Little John.

"Not long," was Robin's reply.

"Somehow we must think of a way to forestall the Sheriff," the giant said. "We must stop him before he can take too stern a revenge on us. Ah, I have a merry notion!"

He jumped up from the table.

"Master, can you arrange to have the Sheriff's dishes set out neatly on the table, ready for a meal?"

"I can," agreed Robin; "but why?"

"And see that the Sheriff's old cook is there to wait on him?"

"That can be arranged also," said Robin. "But I don't understand why, Little John."

"But you will, master," said the giant, smiling; "and before the day is out!"

With that, Little John ran off into the forest, dressed once again in the clothes that the Sheriff of Nottingham had given him whilst he was in his service.

"The Sheriff is bound to return to his castle today," Little John told himself as he ran through the greenwood. "I must be sure to meet him before he reaches his home."

He reached the Nottingham road and waited. Soon, round the bend in the road, he saw the Sheriff riding ahead of his men.

Little John ran from the side of the road and dropped on one knee in front of the Sheriff.

"What are you doing here?" demanded the Sheriff roughly, as he recognised his servant.

"May it please you, sire," said Little John respectfully, "I heard that you would be coming back from your journey today, and I knew that, while you were travelling through the forest, you would be pleased to do some hunting."

"That is for me to say," grunted the Sheriff.

"True, sire," said Little John, "but when I tell you what I have seen I think you will forgive me for coming to meet you."

"Well, varlet, what is it?"

"I saw the largest hart that I have seen in all my life," replied the outlaw. "He was followed by a great herd of deer, which seemed to look upon him as their lord and master."

"H'm!" said the Sheriff, thoughtfully. "Where did you see all this?"

"It was only a mile away from here," said Little John. "If you give me your permission, I shall be pleased to take you to the spot."

"I will go with you," said the Sheriff.

"I can promise fine sport, sire," Little John assured him.

"I shall come alone," said the Sheriff. "My men can return to the castle."

Little John had guessed from the beginning that the Sheriff would not be able to resist hunting this great stag, for he was well known as a keen hunter.

"I shall be glad to see this great beast!" said the Sheriff. "Lead the way, Reynold Greenleaf!"

While the rest of his men went back to the castle, the Sheriff rode forward with Little John.

The outlaw took him through the forest. He ran swiftly, while the Sheriff followed on horseback. Presently they came to a glade, where, under a great tree, sat Robin Hood and his Merrie Men.

The Sheriff turned upon Little John when he realised how he had been trapped; but it was too late.

Robin's men came forward at once and demanded that the Sheriff should dismount.

"This is an honour!" exclaimed Robin, delightedly. "You are very welcome, sire."

"This is an outrage, you mean!" stormed the enraged Sheriff. "You shall pay for this, Robin Hood."

Robin ignored his remark. He was polite in the extreme, but there was a gleam in his eye that made the Sheriff feel very uncomfortable.

Robin showed him the great feast that had been set for him. The Sheriff could do nothing but sit down and eat and drink. He wondered in his heart what Robin Hood would do with him, for it was well known that he had many times vowed to kill Robin Hood.

When the Sheriff saw that all the silver dishes used in the meal were his own he groaned loudly. Then, to make matters worse for him, he looked up and saw his own cook serving out the meal for him. He had a poor appetite that day.

"You have trapped me," he said to Robin Hood. "You have robbed me of my silver, and my own cook has joined you. What are you going to do with me?"

"I think I shall make you wear the same dress as my Merrie Men," laughed Robin.

He ordered his men to take off the Sheriff's clothes and to dress him in Lincoln green. Then he insisted that the Sheriff should stay with them and see how they lived. The Sheriff's protests were of no use. As evening came, Robin made the Sheriff lie down with the men on the hard ground. The Sheriff turned and twisted all night and could get no sleep.

By the time the morning came again he was ready to make Robin any promise he chose.

"You shall stay with us for a year!" declared Robin.

"Robin Hood," replied the Sheriff, "I will do anything but that. I must ask you for mercy."

"Would you have shown me any mercy if you had caught me?" asked Robin pointedly.

"None at all!" said the Sheriff honestly.

"Well, at least you are frank!" smiled the outlaw. He turned to his men. "What shall we do with this man?" he called to them. "We don't want his money, and we don't want his life, as he did ours."

Many of the men said that the Sheriff should be treated as he would have treated Robin if the tables were turned. But Little John stepped forward and addressed the crowd.

"If he had wandered our way and had been caught by us, it would have been different," he said. "But he was brought here through a trick, and we should not kill a man I have led into a trap. We have his silver, and we have his cook. He has learned what merry men we are. Why not make him promise to leave us alone in the future and let him go free?"

They all agreed that this was fair. Robin turned to the Sheriff.

"You came here as our enemy; but we do not wish to take your life. We would rather turn you into a friend. You are in our power, and, as you can see, we could easily kill you; but we will spare you. Yet we think it fair that you should swear friendship to us for ever if we let you go free."

The Sheriff was astonished and relieved.

"It is more than I would have done for you!" he said. "But I see that you are a man, and I will be your friend, as you ask. I shall seek your life no more."

So Robin Hood and his Merrie Men sent away the Sheriff, who kept his promise loyally; but often as he sat at his table and missed all his fine silver he wondered how he could free himself of his promise to Robin.

CHAPTER 20

THE SILVER ARROW

WHEN the Sheriff's wife heard about her husband's adventure with Robin Hood, and how he had made his promise, she was furious. The Sheriff told her how he had been trapped and how lucky he was to be still alive; but it was of no use. His wife would not listen to his excuses, and she did not try to hide from her husband her angry thoughts about him.

"You know very well that Robin Hood is wanted for murder," she cried. "Yet you continue to leave him alone as if he were your friend."

"But I gave him my word that I should leave him alone," replied the Sheriff.

"He will not leave you alone!"

"I cannot go back on my word!" insisted the Sheriff.

"But if I could show you a way to get round your

promise," said his wife craftily, "what would you say to that?"

"If I could set Robin Hood free in the same way that he set me free, I should consider that we were quits," was the Sheriff's answer.

The wife had a plan in her mind, and she told the Sheriff of it.

"All you have to do is to announce a great shooting match in Nottingham. You can rely upon it that Robin Hood will be there if the prize is great enough. You know yourself that there is not a finer archer in the country."

"That's true," admitted the Sheriff. "But I still cannot see how that will free me from my obligations."

"Then listen," went on his wife. "If Robin Hood does come he is sure to win the contest. Let him see that you recognise him when he comes to receive his prize. Secretly order your men to attack him and you yourself allow him to escape before they reach him. You will then be quits."

"It is a cunning plan," admitted the Sheriff. "Then after that I can set out to capture the outlaw and bring him to justice."

The Sheriff made sure that the notices for the shooting contest were posted all over the town. The news of the match spread very quickly, as he had intended, and it was not long before it reached the ears of Robin himself. When Robin learned that the prize was to be a silver arrow, he made up his mind at once.

"The silver arrow will be a fine present for Marian," he announced to his men. "Nothing will keep me from entering the contest."

His men tried to turn him from his bold purpose. They knew that once he was seen in Nottingham he would be captured.

"Has not the Sheriff given me his promise?" asked Robin. "He will not go back on his word."

The outlaws were not so sure about the Sheriff's honesty as was their leader. But Robin told them that he would go in disguise just in case there was any risk.

"On second thoughts," laughed Robin, "I think we must all enter for the contest."

On the day of the match Robin and his men, all in disguise, marched towards Nottingham. Each carried a bow and a number of arrows. As they neared the town they saw that the townspeople were pouring into the meadow where the great shooting match was to be held.

At one end of the meadow a wand, made of willow, was standing up in the ground. This was to be the target. Near this target, special stands had been put up so that the townspeople could have a full view of the competition.

Robin's men mingled with the crowd who were going to shoot, and as there were eight hundred archers taking part they were easily overlooked. On the way to the match Robin decided that only the best of his men would take part in the competition; the remainder would stand by in case of need.

It took a long time for the many contestants to shoot. Gradually the failures dropped out, and at last only five were left in the match. All these five, unknown to the townsfolk, were members of Robin's band.

The Sheriff looked on from his seat in the stand.

"All a waste of time," he muttered to himself. "The great Robin Hood is afraid to show his face here. My stupid wife's plan has just turned out to be a waste of time and expense."

He had no suspicion that the outlaw was not many paces from him.

The five men left in the match were now going to take their final shots. One of them fell out, and then there were four. The four became three, and the three two, until amid cheers, Robin was declared the winner.

He stepped up to receive the prize. As the Sheriff held out the silver arrow to this unknown marksman he suddenly recognised the outlaw. Quivering with excitement, he turned round to whisper something to one of his men—the secret signal that would set the soldiers against Robin Hood. Then he turned back to the outlaw and presented him with the silver arrow.

Suddenly one of the Sheriff's men cried out: "'Tis Robin Hood, the outlaw! Arrest him!"

Soldiers began to swarm towards the stand where Robin Hood stood with the Sheriff.

The Sheriff whispered in Robin's ear.

"Go, Robin Hood, whilst you may! I have kept my promise, but this makes us quits."

Robin saw through the plan at once. He brought out his horn from its hiding-place amongst his clothes and put it to his lips. Immediately the meadow swarmed with the men from Sherwood Forest. They rushed towards the Sheriff's soldiers, and a great battle began. Robin fought his way to the head of his band.

Soon the Sheriff's men were driven back, and

Robin decided that it was time for his men to make their escape into the forest. He called them.

"To the forest, men!" he cried. "Leave these varlets to lick their wounds."

The men turned and ran towards the forest, in whose secret depths lay safety from pursuit.

They had not passed far out of Nottingham when a chance arrow from one of the Sheriff's men embedded itself in Little John's knee. He fell at once. Robin came across the giant as he was trying to pluck the arrow out.

"Pray do not wait for me, master!" said Little John. "Stab me so that I shall not die by the rope. Then leave me."

Robin took no notice of his faithful friend's pleas. He called Much-the-Miller's son, and together they lifted Little John and staggered on with him.

But the Sheriff's men were hot on the heels of the outlaws, and Robin knew that it would not be long before the three of them were overtaken.

"We've only one chance," he said to Much-the-Miller's son. "We must make for Sir Richard of Lea's castle. We could never get as far as the forest before the Sheriff's men overtook us. Sir Richard will give us shelter, I know."

They made their way to the great castle that stood in the distance. Stumbling bravely across fields, they arrived with their burden only a short time before the Sheriff's men.

Sir Richard welcomed them.

"There is no time to be lost," said Sir Richard. "I can see the Sheriff's men in the distance."

"Then help us, Sir Richard, to get Little John to safety."

In a very short time the three outlaws were resting in Sir Richard's castle. The Sheriff's men knew that it would be useless to try and force their way into the great stone fortress. They gave up the chase and returned to Nottingham.

Robin showed his silver-arrow prize to Sir Richard, who said:

"Maid Marian will be very proud of this—and of you."

When at last Robin returned to the forest he presented the prize to his wife. Maid Marian treasured it always, and seldom allowed it out of her sight.

CHAPTER 21

THE CAPTURE OF ROBIN HOOD

"It's stupid!" grumbled Little John, as he sat beneath a tree with Will Scarlet and Much-the-Miller's son.

"What is stupid?"

"The idea our master has of going to Nottingham this morning," answered the giant.

"He has been many times before," Will Scarlet reminded him.

"Yes, but always in disguise. He plans to go to church in Nottingham today without any disguise at all."

Robin was a master of disguise. In a secret forest

lodge he had all sorts of disguises, which he used when occasion demanded. Most of his changes of clothing were bought from their owners in the forest or along the open roads, when needed. Nevertheless, he did not like disguises, and he only used them when he must.

Of all times, Little John considered that going boldly into church was one of those when disguise was vital. Yet Robin had told Little John of his intention to go to church without any disguise at all.

He had refused, to the further annoyance of his best comrade, to be escorted by anybody, obstinately declaring that he wanted, just this once, to go alone.

"Have you no faith in me, Little John?" he asked. "Do not forget that the Sheriff himself promised to leave us unmolested."

But even if Robin trusted the Sheriff, none of his men could believe that they were to be allowed to come and go as they pleased.

However, they could not dissuade Robin from his plan, and on the following Sunday morning he set out early for Nottingham.

It so happened that one of the many monks whom Robin had relieved of money bags in the forest attended the church that morning. The monk recognised Robin straight away, and sent word to the Sheriff.

The Sheriff knew that if he took no action there would be questions asked about his loyalty to the King. He could do nothing but send a party of armed men to capture Robin in the church. Besides, was he not now free to seek the outlaw's capture again?

Half-way through the service there was a loud commotion at the church door. Robin turned to see a party of the Sheriff's men advancing down the aisle towards him. He was on his feet in an instant.

"You varlets!" he cried. "Cannot a man go to church in peace?"

He fought desperately as the Sheriff's men closed in on him. He accounted for a good number before he was dragged down and overpowered through the sheer weight of men against him.

"Oh, that I had taken Little John's advice!" he muttered, as he found himself a prisoner.

He was dragged along to the Sheriff's home. Remembering his promise to Robin, the Sheriff did not have the courage to face him, and he sent word that the outlaw was to be sent to the most distant dungeon and securely chained hand and foot. The Sheriff realised that the King would have to be informed of Robin Hood's capture. That meant that the outlaw would be kept in captivity for some days until the Sheriff's messenger could travel to London and return with the King's orders.

It was the monk himself who offered to go to Westminster with the news of Robin Hood's capture; and that same day he set out alone on the journey from Nottingham to London.

Back in the greenwood camp, Little John called over to where Much-the-Miller's son was preparing some new arrows.

"It is well past the time when our master should be back," he said.

"I was thinking the same," replied the other. "I'm beginning to feel uneasy about him."

"I'm going to Nottingham myself," announced the giant. "I shall soon know if anything is wrong.".

"Wait!" said Much-the-Miller's son. "I will come with you."

The two set out along the Nottingham road. Soon they came to the cottage of one of their friends. There they learned of Robin's capture.

It was while they were talking to the owner of the cottage that they saw, coming along the road from Nottingham, the figure of a mounted monk.

"Ho, Sir Monk!" cried Little John. "Is there any more news of the capture of Robin Hood?"

The monk, who was at this moment on his way to London to take the news to the King, was happy to think that he could take most of the credit for Robin's capture.

"Well," he said, stopping his horse, "the outlaw is captured at last and will meet justice. It was I who first recognised him in the church. And it is I who am taking the news to the King of England for his instructions."

"Bravo!" cried Little John. "But you must be a brave man indeed to venture on such a journey by yourself. What would you do if you were to meet Robin Hood's band along the road?"

"Have no fear," said the monk. "None of his band would know my mission."

Little John gave a knowing wink at Much-the-Miller's son.

"News travels far and quickly," he reminded the monk. "Would you not prefer me and my friend here to accompany you for a way? It is the least we can do to help you."

The monk was grateful for the offer, for he was a

little fearful of meeting outlaws on his way. So the monk was accompanied on his journey by Little John and Much-the-Miller's son.

They travelled for about a mile, when the road became very lonely and deserted.

Much-the-Miller's son whispered to Little John that the time had come to end the monk's journey to London. They rode on for a short distance farther. Then they attacked.

The monk had no time to wonder what it all meant, for Little John jumped upon his back, dragging him off his horse. He pulled the cowl down over the monk's face, and tied him up. Then they escorted him, blindfold, through the secret paths of Sherwood Forest to their greenwood home, where they left him in charge of faithful followers of Robin Hood.

CHAPTER 22

THE RESCUE OF ROBIN HOOD

ONE EVENING, a week after Robin Hood had been taken prisoner, two travellers called at the Sheriff's house. The Sheriff had been a worried man since Robin was taken prisoner. Every night the outlaw's friends had made attempts to release him, but they had not succeeded.

When he heard that two travellers had arrived from Westminster, the Sheriff felt relieved. He showed them into his dining-room at once.

Little John kept in the shadows of the hall so that the Sheriff would not recognise him. He had to take care, for he had served the Sheriff under the name of Reynold Greenleaf.

Much-the-Miller's son handed the Sheriff a letter supposed to be from the King of England.

"Where is the monk who took the letter to the King?" asked the Sheriff.

"The King took such a fancy to him that he kept him in London," replied Much-the-Miller's son.

The Sheriff asked no further questions, but studied the King's message.

The King ordered that Robin should be taken to London. The Sheriff invited his guests to eat and drink with him while they discussed the best way of getting their dangerous prisoner to London. As soon as the servants had left the room, however, Little John clapped his great hand over the Sheriff's mouth, so that he could not cry out, while Much-the-Miller's son tied him securely to his chair. Then the two bold outlaws left him, and made their way out of the castle.

They ran silently through the streets and down dark alleys. They intended to find Robin's cell to see what chance there was of helping him to escape. Such a strong guard had been placed around the gates of Nottingham that none of Robin's band had yet been able to get inside the city to free their outlaw leader. Little John and Much-the-Miller's son now had a chance of rescue.

Before long they came to an open space and found that they were walking across country ground. They were between the town walls and the castle rock. It was somewhere in the side of the castle rock, as Little

John had discovered, that there was an entrance to a cave. At the end of this cave lay the dungeon in which Robin Hood was kept prisoner whilst the Sheriff awaited the return of the messengers from Westminster.

It was Much-the-Miller's son who stumbled across the cave entrance. It was half covered by leafy bushes. At the sound of his stumbling a sentry came running to the cave-mouth. He had no time to cry out before Little John leapt from the shadows and felled him with a single blow.

The two men ran swiftly into the cave, slowing up as the light became more dim. Presently they came to a door. It was locked.

"Stand clear!" said Little John, and charged the door.

Under his great weight, the door gave way, and the two hurried on. In front of them was a long flight of stone steps, at the top of which stood a sentry.

"Ho, sentry!" called Little John from the darkness at the bottom of the steps.

The sentry turned, grasped one of the torches that were burning in the wall at the top of the steps, and started to make his way down the steps.

Little John waited, then delivered a blow that felled the sentry like a log. He lay still at the foot of the stairs.

Other voices could now be heard. Little John had made more noise than was safe. Heavy footsteps sounded at the top of the stairs. There was no time to be lost.

"Help, there!" cried Little John loudly. "Robin Hood has escaped!"

The footsteps broke into a run.

"Which way did he go?" asked the voice of another sentry excitedly.

It was too dark where Little John was standing for the sentry to see him. He called out that Robin Hood had run down the stairs and along the passage that led out of the castle rock. The sentry ran on. A second guard followed him. A third started to do the same, but, instead, he ran to a cell door, and knocked heavily upon it.

"Hallo! What's ado now?"

Little John heard the voice from the inside of the cell. It was the voice of Robin Hood!

"Whoever has escaped, 'tis not Robin Hood!" cried the sentry.

"Not yet," smiled Little John, as he struck the sentry a blow that sent him reeling to the ground.

He picked up the keys that had been left lying by the side of the first warder. He found one that fitted the cell lock, and thrust open the heavy wooden door.

Little John walked in.

"Bravely done!" commented a calm voice. "Loosen my chains, and I will do my part."

Much-the-Miller's son brought over the bunch of keys, and tried them until he had opened the padlocks that bound Robin's chains. Robin stood up and stretched his cramped body. It was great to be unfettered again.

Suddenly there came the sound of men rushing towards the cell door. Robin and his two companions stood by the door silently. The cell was dark. One, two, three, four men, with swords, rushed into the cell.

Robin dragged Little John and Much-the-Miller's son out of the door. Once free, he slammed the door quickly shut, and locked it. The four soldiers were imprisoned before they realised what was happening.

"How shall we get out of here, Robin?" asked Little John.

"I shall go out as I came in," said Robin; "by the Great Entrance."

His plan was a daring one. They marched out boldly with a score of other men who were ordered to raise the Town Guard and warn all the warders at the gates.

There was one dangerous moment when a big soldier, hurrying to find out what the commotion was about, bumped against Little John. The giant outlaw, thinking that he was discovered, promptly grappled with the soldier and threw him.

"Hey, what means this?" cried the soldier angrily.

"He thought you wished to try your strength against his," cried Robin quickly, seeing that Little John had made a mistake. "Your pardon, friend!"

All who met Robin and his friends after that took them to be some of the soldiers that had been called in from Wakefield and Pontefract to make the garrison larger.

Robin Hood was a free man again.

CHAPTER 23

TWO STRONG WILLS

ROBIN was walking along the Nottingham road one day when he saw coming towards him two men.

"Good afternoon!" said Robin to the men.

"I have no use for fellows who bow and scrape to me," said one of the men to Robin.

Robin was angered by the fellow's tone.

"Civility costs nothing," said he.

The man looked at Robin, as if to inquire what sort of man he was that should dare answer him back.

"Any more insolence from you," said the man, "and I shall knock your head off!"

"You are welcome to try," said Robin.

He was not afraid of these two men. Many times had he had encounters with such ruffians, but he had always been able to give a good account of himself.

"Take care!" said the other man. "We are messengers from the Bishop of Hereford. We are on our way to Nottingham to deliver a message to the Sheriff. We do not intend to be hindered by such as you."

"But you are hindered, you see," replied Robin, with a smile; "and, what is more, you are going to spend the night with me."

The two men laughed. Just then Little John came up and asked Robin if he was having trouble. Robin told him that the two men were to spend the night with them, and Little John wasted no time in tackling one of the men. Robin went for the other. With their superior strength and training, the outlaws were soon escorting the two men back to camp.

An idea was building itself up in Robin's mind. Before they had reached the camp, he made plans for a new adventure.

The men were given food and then made to lie down with the rest of Robin's men and so spend the night with them.

Early next morning, Robin called Will Scarlet and Will Gamwell.

"How would you like to carry out a dangerous piece of work for me?" asked Robin.

The two Wills were keen at once.

"What do you want us to do, Robin?" asked Will Gamwell.

"I have read the letter that those two messengers were taking to the Sheriff of Nottingham. In it the Bishop of Hereford is asking for a loan of two hundred pounds. He says that it is urgent and very important. Do you think that you two could impersonate the two messengers and go to the Sheriff with this letter? It would be such fun to disappoint the Bishop, and at the same time to score one against the Sheriff of Nottingham."

The eyes of the two Wills glistened.

They changed clothes with the two messengers, and with the letter set out for the Sheriff's castle. They arrived at Nottingham in the early afternoon and went straight to the Sheriff. He read the letter in silence.

"Two hundred pounds is a lot of money," he said. "If I scraped together all the money I have with me I doubt whether it would total that amount."

"Then we had better take as much money as you can gather," said Will Scarlet. "The Bishop will be very angry if we go back with nothing."

The Sheriff at length agreed to gather as much money as he could, and collected altogether a hundred and fifty pounds. He gave this money to the two men.

"Be very careful," he told them. "There are men in Sherwood Forest who would not hesitate to rob you of all your money if they caught you. They are led by Robin Hood, the outlaw."

"We have heard of him," said Will Gamwell. "We have no fear of being caught and robbed."

They thanked the Sheriff, and walked out of his room. On reaching the gate, they came face to face with the Bishop of Hereford! The Bishop had come to the Sheriff personally because he was so much in need of the money that, after his messengers had set out, he thought a personal visit would make more certain of the needed loan.

The two Wills did not wait. They took to their heels and ran out of the gate. But they had not gone far before the Sheriff learned from the Bishop's own lips that the two men were impostors. At once, the Sheriff, with his men, set out to catch the two fugitives.

"We shall never be able to get back to the forest," said Will Scarlet.

"Let us try to reach Sir Richard of Lea's castle," panted Will Gamwell.

The two men ran in the direction of Sir Richard's stronghold, and came at last to the gate. Sir Richard welcomed them, as men of Robin Hood's band. He had not forgotten the kindness shown him when he fell on hard times.

Not far behind the two runaways was the Sheriff. He called his men to the castle. There he decided to attack the main gate. He took his men some distance away to consider the best way of launching the assault.

Sir Richard guessed what his enemy intended to do. So he ordered that the planks of the drawbridge should be loosened so that they were just resting on their cross-supports. The drawbridge was to be left down.

All this was quickly done.

A few minutes later, a great force of the Sheriff's men charged towards the drawbridge. The Sheriff and the Bishop were in the lead. The Bishop had come racing up when he first saw the chase, and he had now joined in the fray.

They saw that the drawbridge had been left down, and thought that someone had blundered, for it was natural that it should be pulled up at the first sign of attack.

The Sheriff and the Bishop raced across the bridge, followed closely by the first of the force. From inside the castle Sir Richard's men began to raise the draw-bridge. As the great structure rose upwards, the loosened boards began to slip. Very soon, as the angle of the bridge became steeper, the boards, with nothing to hold them, began to slide right off the bridge. With a great splash, they slid into the moat below. The mass of men on the bridge went down with them!

The Sheriff and the Bishop, who had reached the end of the drawbridge, were able to cling to the great iron gate and thus save themselves from falling into the water. They looked rather like monkeys hanging on to the gate.

Will Scarlet, inside the castle, had made a great bucket of paste. Together he and Will Gamwell carried it to the room above the drawbridge and watched what was going on through the holes that were always bored in the floors of these chambers.

When they saw what had happened to the Sheriff and the Bishop, they poured the great bucket of sticky paste through the holes in the floor, right on to the heads of the two struggling men below.

The proud Bishop and the haughty Sheriff were smothered in the wet, sticky mass, which forced them to loosen their hold on the gate and slide down into the water.

Those inside the castle roared with laughter.

All thoughts of money were forgotten for the moment by the Sheriff and the Bishop. Their one concern was to reach dry land. They swam as strongly as they could for the far bank. Once upon dry land they ran as fast as they could towards the Sheriff's own castle. They had had enough for one day!

The two Wills dined with Sir Richard, and, after thanking him for his kindness in helping them to escape, they made their way back to Robin Hood and his Merrie Men.

CHAPTER 24

RESCUE FROM THE ROPE

THE SHERIFF had been quick to act. As soon as he reached home, he proclaimed that the price on Robin Hood's head was doubled. He was still dripping with paste, and he thought that no price would be too high to pay for vengeance on the gay outlaw of Sherwood Forest.

At the news, a band of men armed themselves and set out for the forest, where they knew the outlaws lived. They needed money and they could think of no better way of getting a large sum than to bring back Robin Hood.

Robin was away from his band the morning the attack was planned. He had gone visiting with Marian, and had told his men that he would not be back until nightfall.

"There's a great crowd of men coming towards us!" exclaimed Will Scarlet, peering through the trees. "It looks like trouble ahead!"

The outlaws made ready to face the attack. So many of their members were out on hunting expeditions that there were not enough left in the camp to defend it properly. Those that were there put up a brave show.

The band of men who were advancing knew that they would be no match for the outlaws if they

fought man to man. Their only chance was to wound
some of the men from a distance. And that is what
they did. They kept as far away from Robin's men
as they could and shot arrows towards the figures in
Lincoln green. Three of the outlaws fell. They
were Will the Wrestler and his two brothers, Lester
and Harry.

This was enough for the band of men. They
captured the three men and made their way back
through the forest as quickly as they could. Though
there were many more of them than there were outlaws in the camp, they did not fancy staying to fight
it out, for they feared the skill of the men in green.

"Even if we haven't got Robin Hood," said the
leader of the men, "at least we should get some
reward for these three specimens."

The men laughed. They knew how anxious the
Sheriff was to recover his good name after the fiasco
of Robin's imprisonment. He would welcome the
capture of these three outlaws.

When the Sheriff saw three of Robin's men he was
delighted.

"They shall be hanged tomorrow," he announced.
"A public hanging will serve as a warning to Robin
Hood that I mean business this time."

Robin was upset when he heard about the capture
of the three brothers. He had only been back at the
camp for a short time when an old lady came through
the forest and asked to see him. She was a poor
widow, the mother of the three brothers who had
been captured.

"Good Robin Hood," she began, "my three sons
have this day been captured and are to hang tomorrow. I beg you to save them for me. They are all I

have in this world. Though they were in your band, they often visited me, and they always saw that I had enough to live on."

Robin assured the widow that he would do all he could to rescue the three brothers.

Early next day he set out along the road to Nottingham. He saw the figure of a palmer in front of him, and quickly caught up with the old man.

"Where are you going, honest palmer?" asked Robin.

"To Nottingham," replied the palmer. "Three brave men are to hang today. They shall not die until I have prayed with them."

Robin had a sudden inspiration. He begged the palmer to exchange clothes with him so that he could go to the hanging. The palmer would not hear of such a scheme as Robin outlined, but the jingle of money seemed to work a quick change in him. In less than an hour, Robin was passing through the city gate of Nottingham in the guise of a palmer.

He made his way straight to the scaffold. The three brothers were standing there bound and made ready for the hanging.

"Good Sheriff," cried the palmer, "it is surely right that these three varlets should be given the opportunity of repenting before they die."

"They'll have plenty of time for that," returned the Sheriff. "I can get nobody to hang them!"

"Then give me permission to carry out the executions," pleaded the palmer. "Justice must be done."

There was relief on the Sheriff's face when he heard this. The crowd jeered the palmer as he stepped on the platform. But the Sheriff was pleased that he need no longer fear ridicule for failing at the last moment to carry out his sentence.

The palmer was speaking now to the three condemned men. Little did the Sheriff know what he was saying.

"It is your leader," whispered Robin. "Have no fear, I'll loosen your bonds, and then, when I give the word, we must fight our way out of here."

Their bonds were at last loosened, but the men stood still, pretending that they were still tied.

Suddenly Robin threw off his palmer's robes and stood revealed in Lincoln green. He put his horn to his lips, and blew three sharp blasts. In a few moments men began to pour through the distant trees towards the execution-place. The outlaws had again answered the call of their beloved leader.

"Run for it!" cried Robin to the three brothers. "Fight for your lives!"

The three men, with Robin at their head, battled their way out of the crowd with their fists. The Sheriff's men gathered quickly together and awaited orders; but they had lost too much time, for Robin and the three brothers were running towards their friends in Lincoln green, who were now near the scene.

Desperately the Sheriff lined up his men.

"Your weapons!" he cried. "Where are your weapons?"

"We laid them in a heap on the ground just before the execution was due to take place," said one man.

"Then get them, varlets, get them!" stormed the Sheriff.

The men broke ranks and ran to retrieve their spears and swords. They began to line up again.

Escape was complete by the time the Sheriff and his men were properly mustered. Robin's men far outnumbered the few soldiers that had gathered to watch the execution, and the Sheriff could do nothing but look on hopelessly at the distant figures who were vanishing quickly in the direction of far-away Sherwood Forest.

CHAPTER 25

THE MERRY WIDOW

WHEN Widow Hardlock saw her three sons safe she was indeed grateful to Robin.

Deep in the greenwood, Robin was hunting on his own for the greater part of the day. Suddenly, without any sound, the Bishop of Hereford came upon him.

"Stand still, Robin Hood!" the Bishop commanded in a loud voice, dismounting swiftly from his horse. "I have a debt to pay you."

The Bishop could never forget how Robin Hood had cheated him out of the loan he had sought from the Sheriff of Nottingham. He hoped that now would be his chance to make matters even.

"Good-day, good Bishop!" laughed Robin, turning to face the portly gentleman. "I'm always ready to accept a debt; more especially one that will carry with it your blessing."

E

"This is no laughing matter," said the Bishop. "You once robbed me of a sum of money loaned to me by the Sheriff of Nottingham, but now I vow I'll rob you of your laugh!"

"Oh, come!" returned Robin, genially. "I've been hunting one of the finest specimens of the King's deer I'm ever likely to see. Join me, good Bishop, and perhaps your influence will cause the deer to repent of his fast-moving ways and allow me to catch him."

"You know full well that it is a grave offence to kill the King's deer," raged the Bishop. "I'm glad I have caught you in the act of chasing them. You will rue this day."

"I am sorry," sighed Robin. "If you are in that mood I cannot put up with you. We must go our own ways."

Robin started to walk away, when, looking back, he saw the Bishop remount his horse to give chase. Robin had no wish to harm the Bishop, and he felt like having fun, so he ran off through the undergrowth as fast as he could. But he had no chance against a swift-footed horse, which quickly overtook him.

Robin then decided to run in amongst the trees, where the horse could not easily follow. As he broke through the undergrowth, he saw a cottage standing amongst the trees. It was Widow Hardlock's home. Robin knew that he would get a welcome there; so he opened the cottage door.

"Good dame," he cried to Widow Hardlock, "I must hide at once, for the Bishop of Hereford is hot on my trail."

It was not long before the Bishop saw the cottage

standing in the greenwood. He steered his horse towards it, and knocked loudly on the door.

"Come in," called a voice.

"Ah," began the Bishop, eyeing the old widow, who was working peacefully at her loom. "Have you seen anything of an outlaw dressed in Lincoln green, old dame?"

"No, good Bishop," she answered; "but look around yourself. He may be in hiding."

The Bishop started a search of her cottage. Suddenly he heard a movement in one of the cupboards. He flung open the door, and there, huddling in a corner, was Robin Hood.

"Out with you!" cried the Bishop, excitedly.

The trapped man walked out of the cupboard, offering no resistance. He was led away by the Bishop, leaving the old widow working once more at her loom.

Back in the forest, Little John and Will Scarlet were walking together towards the outlaws' camp when they heard a rustle behind them. Coming towards them was a strange figure in black.

"Why, it's Widow Hardlock!" exclaimed Little John.

"No, it is not," said the figure. "Little John, don't you know your master when you see him?"

Little John burst out laughing. Will Scarlet joined him. To see their master dressed in those odd garments was indeed a funny sight.

Robin quickly explained that he had been chased by the Bishop of Hereford in the forest, and, taking refuge in Widow Hardlock's cottage, he had quickly changed clothes with her. The widow had hidden in a cupboard, so that when the Bishop searched he thought he had found the outlaw.

"If he had known that it was Robin Hood sitting at the loom he would not have been so courteous," laughed Robin.

Three blasts on his horn brought Robin's men around him. He changed clothes with one of the new members of the band, and led his merry men through forest-paths in the direction of Nottingham, where he hoped to cut across the route taken by the Bishop and his captive.

"There he is!" cried Robin, as they emerged from the forest on to the Nottingham road.

They soon caught up with the Bishop and brought him to a halt.

"What is this?" began the outraged Bishop, as he looked at Robin and then at the old lady dressed in Lincoln green.

He was so bewildered that Robin Hood could hardly keep from laughter.

"My good Bishop," said Robin, advancing towards him, "what sort of outrage is it when you grab an innocent old lady and take her by force away from her cottage?"

"But you . . ." began the Bishop.

"Widow Hardlock," cut in Robin, "I think the Bishop deserves a box on the ears for his rudeness."

Widow Hardlock thought so too. With a twinkle in her eyes she smote the Bishop heartily over his ears.

"You have wasted a great deal of this woman's time," said Robin to the Bishop. "The money she has lost from her work must be made up."

He ordered the Bishop to pay the widow the exact amount of money she would have made had she been working all the time. Then he allowed the Bishop to go on his way.

"You must be our guest of honour at a feast in the forest tonight," said Robin, as he escorted the widow back to the forest encampment.

CHAPTER 26

THE BOGGED BISHOP

WHEN HE arrived home, the Bishop was in an ill humour. Once again Robin Hood had scored against him. Was there no law in this land? The Bishop decided that, if the Sheriff could not catch the outlaw, he would take a great number of men with him and capture the man without the Sheriff's aid. There would be no slip this time.

On a bright summer's morning about a week after his adventure with Widow Hardlock, the Bishop of Hereford set out towards the forest with fifty armed men. The trouble was that he was not sure exactly where Robin Hood had his encampment. He wandered in the direction where he had seen the outlaw the previous week.

Coming through the forest were two rough-looking tramps. The Bishop rode ahead of his men and spoke to them.

"Do you want the price of a meal, my good men?" he asked in a friendly manner.

One tramp looked at the other.

"What say you, Will?" There was a twinkle in Little John's eye as he spoke. Disguised as a couple of tramps, he and Will Scarlet had set out that morning in search of adventure, and before they had gone far it seemed that adventure had come to them. He turned to the Bishop, saying: "Why, yes, good Bishop. My friend and I have not eaten for two whole days."

"Then tell me, if you can, where Robin Hood, the outlaw, has his camp."

The Bishop knew that many of the vagabonds were friendly with the outlaws and knew his whereabouts.

Will Scarlet and Little John set him off in the wrong direction and ran back through the forest to tell Robin of what had taken place.

"We'll teach the Bishop a lesson that he will never forget!" exclaimed Robin.

Quickly gathering together a number of his men, he led them through the forest in the direction the Bishop had gone. Before long they could see the tail end of the fifty men who were riding behind the Bishop.

"This is better than I had hoped!" laughed Robin. "If the Bishop would only turn a little more to the left he would lead his men straight into the muddy swamp."

All of a sudden Robin saw how he could put the swamp to good use.

"Come!" he cried. "Let us head the Bishop off. When he sees us, we will pretend to run away from him."

The Bishop was delighted when he saw Robin and

a number of his men emerge from the forest. It looked as if the outlaw had seen the Bishop, too, for he suddenly stopped, turned his men about, and ran off again into the forest.

"After them, men!" screamed the Bishop excitedly. "They must not escape!"

Robin led his men in a great circle round the edges of the swamp. The Bishop thought that by charging straight ahead he could quickly cut off the outlaws. He led his men forward with a great rush. He wasn't prepared for the shocks he was to experience in the next moments.

He had covered only about twenty yards when his horse floundered in the mud and threw him off. Up he staggered and tried to run forward to get out of the mire; but at each step he became more deeply embedded, and before he had time to turn back he was up to his knees in the swamp.

The fifty men saw the Bishop's plight and stopped on the edge. They could see the uselessness of going any further. Robin Hood's men were covering them with their longbows from the other side of the swamp, so the riders turned their horses round and fled into the forest. The Bishop was left floundering around in the mud on his own.

His frenzied efforts to clamber on to dry land only made his plight worse. Before long the mud reached to his armpits.

"Save me, Robin Hood!" he pleaded frantically. "Save me, and I will cause you no more trouble!"

Robin ordered his men to bring up logs. Placing these on the swamp, two of the men crawled along them to the Bishop. Slowly they hauled him out of the sucking morass. He looked a very sorry sight indeed. From his shoulders to his feet he was one mass of oozing mud.

The outlaws carried him back through the forest to their camp. After lighting a great fire, they sent him to wash while his clothes were being dried. They were useless, however, for the mud had ruined the garments, and the Bishop had to dress in Lincoln green like the outlaws.

"You must be starving," said Robin, without a trace of malice or ill-feeling in his voice. "I know you will join us in a feast."

The Bishop had no wish to offend Robin further. He was thankful to be alive. He agreed that he was hungry.

"Then you must eat with us," laughed Robin again. "We have some of the finest of the King's meat you could ever wish to taste."

When the Bishop saw the great feast that was being brought to the long trestle-tables set up in the greenwood his mouth watered. Maid Marian had made a special point of seeing that the meal on this day was served up in a royal manner. But when the Bishop realised that he was to eat the King's venison he was not sure that his appetite was quite so keen as he had thought.

The delicious smell of the cooked meat soon set his conscience at rest, however, and he ate as heartily as any man. It was late that night before the Bishop was set on his horse and escorted to the edge of the forest, homeward-bound.

CHAPTER 27

ALAN-A-DALE'S WEDDING

"Let us take a walk through the forest," suggested Robin one quiet summer evening.

"You have more energy than six men put together," laughed Maid Marian, as she finished the last patch on one of the outlaw's suits.

Together they set out through the greenwood, drinking in the sounds and scents of the forest, which shone green and gold in the evening sunlight.

"It's good to be alive on an evening like this," said Maid Marian, happily.

"Hark!" cried Robin suddenly. "It sounds as if someone in the forest agrees with you."

From a short distance ahead came the musical sound of a well-trained baritone voice, singing a gay ballad of the day. There seemed to be a hush over the woodland while the voice sang out, as if the animals and birds were listening enraptured.

Robin and Marian walked in the direction of the merry notes. They crossed the border of beech-trees that formed the line of a clearing in the forest. Walking gaily along on the other side of the open space was a young man. He had a stick in his hand, which at every pause in his song he would swish merrily through the air.

Robin pulled Marian back behind a tree as the young man half turned; but he had not seen them, and he walked carelessly onwards, to vanish a moment later into the belt of trees.

"There is a happy young man for you," cried Robin, "one without a care in the world!"

They wandered off in a different direction and took a roundabout route back to the camp.

A week later the two were walking again in the same direction when they saw once more the merry youth whose song had rung through the forest. Now, however, he was lying full length in the grass, silent and sad. Only his bright orange hose betrayed him to Robin and Marian as they wandered into the clearing.

"Perhaps he knows no more songs," whispered Robin, glancing at him.

"There's something strangely sorrowful about him," replied Maid Marian.

Robin and Marian walked towards the youth. At the sound of their footsteps he sprang up, eyeing them with suspicion.

"What do you want?" he demanded.

"We want nothing," returned Robin; "but you looked so dejected lying there that we wished to know if aught ailed you. Only a week ago we saw you here, singing heartily, as if you hadn't a care at all. Yet today it would seem that all the trouble in the world has fallen upon your shoulders."

"If you want to know," said the youth, none too politely, "there is woe enough in my heart."

"Can we help you?"

"No, there is no one who can help me." Then, as if repenting of his manner, he went on: "A week

ago I was going to marry a very beautiful maiden.
Ellen is her name. We were planning to be married
soon. The world was indeed a gay and happy place.
Then, this morning, came the dreadful news that
tomorrow Ellen must marry a Norman baron."

"And is the Lady Ellen in love with the baron?"
asked Maid Marian, in her practical way.

"Madam, she is as heartbroken as I."

"I don't understand," put in Robin. "Tell us
more of this, young man. First, what is your name?"

"Men call me Alan-a-Dale," answered the youth.

"And why is the Lady Ellen going to marry the
baron?"

"Her father has fallen on hard times," explained
Alan-a-Dale. "The Norman baron is rich, and he has
offered a large sum of money if Ellen's father will give
him his daughter's hand."

"And so poor Ellen will be married to this baron
just because the father is in need of money!" exclaimed
Maid Marian. "It is a shameful bargain!"

"Where is the wedding to take place?" asked Robin.

"At an abbey near Nottingham."

"Robin," pleaded Maid Marian, "we must help
this young man. We can't let two young people in
love be parted to please the whim of an autocratic
Norman. We must act."

"We will," said Robin. With a determined air, he
turned again to Alan-a-Dale. "Have no fear," he said.
"The wedding shall be stopped tomorrow. But there
is a price. The price shall be that you join my band
of outlaws, if Ellen is willing. She would be right
good company for Marian."

"I guessed you were Robin Hood," said the young
man. "I give you my oath on your demand, for I

would have joined you anyway if the marriage had taken place between Ellen and the baron."

"Then come back to my camp with me," Robin invited him. "I will introduce you to my good comrades."

The three walked back to Robin's camp. Robin gathered his men about him, and when they were all seated told them the story of Alan-a-Dale and his lady-love. The outlaws were keen to know how their leader planned to stop the wedding on the following day; but Robin had not then worked out a plan. Later, he sat apart from his band, and thought deeply.

Early the next morning the Abbey bells pealed out loudly, announcing the wedding to all the townsfolk. Later, inside the Abbey, all the seats were full. Such a large congregation had never before been seen in the old building. Few guessed, however, that it wasn't so much the townspeople's desire to see the marriage as the fact that Robin Hood's men were there in force, disguised as ordinary folk, that swelled the congregation to such an extent.

"Here she comes, now!" the whisper ran round the crowd.

All eyes were turned to the doorway as Ellen, beautiful in her white wedding gown, entered. She was sad at heart and found it hard to smile. She knew her life was being sacrificed to the Norman baron's gold.

A rough, dirty-looking individual thrust himself towards her and her father, who was accompanying her down the aisle.

"I come to bring the maiden luck," laughed the rough-looking fellow.

It was often considered lucky for a tramp or a chimney-sweep to be present at a wedding. The three walked up to the altar, where the baron was waiting. His thin lips tightened as he saw the rough vagabond. Impertinent fellow! How dare he accost his future bride? The three figures reached his side. This was not the place to make a scene. The baron remained silent, and beamed at his bride-to-be.

Suddenly he cried out: "Take your hand from me!"

The beam had died on the baron's face, and he shouted loudly as the tramp grabbed him by the scruff of his neck.

"Stand aside," ordered the vagabond, roughly, throwing off his clothes and revealing a suit of Lincoln green.

It was Robin Hood!

Robin faced his men in the congregation and beckoned them to him. They ran to him from all parts of the Abbey.

To the amazement of the Bishop, who was standing ready to perform the ceremony, Robin raised his horn to his lips. Immediately, six archers appeared at the doorway, each with his bow at the ready. They made way for the entrance of a lone figure. He marched lightly down the aisle. It was Alan-a-Dale. As Ellen recognised him, she gave a cry of delight.

"My Lord Bishop," said Robin, loudly, so that everyone in the Abbey could hear, "you were about to marry together two people who would never have been happy. The bride shall marry the person she loves. Ask her who that is!"

"This is most irregular——" began the outraged Bishop.

"Ask her!" repeated Robin.

"Well, who is it?" asked the Bishop, nervously, turning to Ellen.

"Alan-a-Dale is the man I love," replied Ellen, without hesitation.

"Then I cannot perform the ceremony," blustered the Bishop. "I have never been so——"

"That is all right," cut in Robin. "Forward, men!"

Robin's men pushed the infuriated Bishop aside. He struggled to free himself, and two of the outlaws sat on him to keep him quiet.

"The good Friar Tuck shall perform the ceremony," said Robin.

The fat friar ambled down the aisle, with a benign smile on his face. He smiled at Robin, smiled at the Bishop, who was red in the face at the indignity of being sat on, and turned to the two lovers standing before him.

Alan-a-Dale and Ellen were married at once. They embraced each other in happy contentment as they became man and wife. What had looked like being a great tragedy ended happily, after all.

CHAPTER 28

ROBIN HOOD AT SEA

ONE VERY cold autumn Robin and Marian, hardened though they were to all weathers in the greenwood, found life in Sherwood Forest hard to bear.

As the coming winter was likely to be severe, they decided that they would move elsewhere until the warmer weather came.

The forest scene changed to leafless, rainswept coldness. Many of the outlaws returned secretly to their homes to spend the winter by the warmth of their cottage fires. Robin and Marian made ready at last to travel far away to somewhere where they would not be known.

"I have a mind to try the sea," said Robin.

"I can't imagine you as a sailor," laughed Marian.

"Well, at least it will be something I haven't yet tackled," replied the outlaw.

They travelled to an obscure fishing-village on the east coast. Under the name of Simon-from-over-the-Lee, Robin searched for lodgings for himself and Maid Marian.

"We are poor fisherfolk from the south," he explained to the widow who opened her door to their knock.

The widow was in need of money, and she took in the two lodgers. Both Robin and Marian were used to hard work, and they gladly set about helping the widow with her daily chores. She grew fond of her two willing helpers. Soon she was satisfied that Robin was honest.

"I have a fishing-boat," she said to him one evening. "My husband left it to me when he died. I've lent the boat out to many local fishermen, but they are dishonest. They cheat me out of my share of the profits. Yet what can I do? I am in no position to argue, for they are men."

Robin was full of sympathy for the woman. He realised how handicapped she was. Yet he half regretted showing his feelings, for her next statement gave him a shock.

"You are a fisherman," she said, eyeing him. "I would be very willing to let you use my boat. I know I can trust you, young man, to see that I am given my fair share of the profits."

Robin looked at Marian. She knew what was passing through his mind at that moment. How could they tell the widow that their story of being fisherfolk was merely made up in order to get lodgings? There was nothing for it but to face up to the situation.

"After all," said Robin when he and Marian were alone, "there's nothing a man cannot do if he tries."

"But, Robin, you haven't the faintest idea of how to manage a boat!"

"No; but I could sail with the present crew and keep an eye on them. At the same time, I could learn by watching."

Robin sailed in the boat the next day. They were well out into the fishing-grounds when the crew cast their lines into the sea. All of them carefully placed their baits at the ends of their lines and sat quietly down, watching—all, that is, except Robin. He had no bait. He cast his empty line into the sea and copied the crew in their patient vigil.

"Hey, Cap'n!" called one of the crew.

The skipper of the boat came up to the man.

"This new fellow, here," he said, pointing to Robin, "calls himself a fisherman. Ask him how many fish he'll catch without using any bait!"

The crew laughed at this. They chuckled at the simpleton who sat amongst them; but the captain did not share their mirth.

"He's wasting his time," he declared. "What's more, he's wasting my time also."

He walked over to where Robin sat staring seriously at his line, as if he were expecting a fish to bite at any moment.

"D'you call yourself a fisherman, Simon-from-over-the-Lee?" he grumbled, raising his voice. "It's hard work for all on this ship. Everyone must carry an equal share of responsibility."

"Responsibility!" repeated Robin. "I'm as anxious as anybody to catch fish."

"Then try baiting your line," thundered the enraged skipper. "It'll be a long time before you thrive at sea. I promise you that you shan't share in our catch."

Robin drew in his line, and looked straight at the skipper.

"I'm sorry for the day I came to these parts," he said. "I wish I were in Sherwood Forest, chasing the deer."

The skipper jeered at him.

"I beg your pardon, your lordship," he said, sarcastically. "I'm afraid we can offer you only our humble fishing-boat. You should go to Sherwood Forest and join Robin Hood!"

Robin smiled to himself, but said nothing.

Later in the day the skipper came round again. He made many minor adjustments to the ship's fittings, tightening something here, removing something there.

"You will long more than ever to be on dry land shortly," he sneered at Robin. "A great storm is blowing up."

Robin shuddered inwardly. He looked at the

ominous sky above him. He had heard all about storms at sea. They were not very pleasant. He shrugged his shoulders. There was nothing he could do about it.

Before the day was out, the ship was tossing helplessly in a great storm. Much of the ship's equipment was swept overboard by the roaring waters. Robin was no sailor, and he longed to be on dry land as he watched the small boat tossing crazily on the swirling sea. For three days the storm raged. Many times the crew thought that they would all be lost as the ship plunged and reared and rocked.

On the fourth day the sea became suddenly calm. Robin was amazed at the suddenness with which the storm abated. Nobody aboard had the faintest notion of where they were. Neither was there any time now to work their bearings out on the chart, for swooping down upon them was a ship of war. It was a French pirate ship.

The skipper of the fishing-boat was horrified.

"Every fish we have on board will be lost," he said. "We shall all be killed or taken as slaves."

"Not on your life!" spoke up Robin. "Give me my bow and arrows. Not a Frenchman will I spare."

"Hold your tongue, you conceited landlubber," stormed the skipper. "I've half a mind to throw you into the sea to lighten our load. We were never in this plight before. You are a bad influence on the boat."

Robin laughed. He stood up in the ship, and drew his trusty bow. An arrow sped upwards. Almost immediately a man from the pirate vessel crumpled to his knees. Robin fitted another arrow, and another.

As each flew towards the pirate ship, it carried death with it. Men slumped to the decks; some crashed into the sea.

"Master!" cried Robin to the skipper of the fishing-boat. "Don't flee from the pirate ship. There aren't many men aboard her; and those that are left are not very cunning."

The skipper was speechless for a moment. That this useless fisherman should be such a wonderful marksman with his bow was astonishing to him. He had never seen such accurate shooting; but could the archer, marvellous though he was, kill all the pirates? It would not only be a great feat—it would be something quite unheard-of, unbelievable. He wheeled round on Robin.

"I take back all I said ill of you," he apologised. "You may not be a good fisherman, but you are a brave and clever man."

"This is no time for apologies, Skipper," cried Robin. "Tie me to the mast so that I shall not slip. I can shoot straight with my bow, but I am not so sure-footed on this rocking boat."

"Get some rope," the skipper called to two of his men. "Lash this man to the mast, so that he doesn't fall."

Simon-from-over-the-Lee was soon bound to the mast, where he could then concentrate fully on the men in the pirate ship. His arrows flew straight into the hearts of the Frenchmen. One by one they fell.

"Great shooting!" cried the fishing-boat skipper, delightedly.

At last Robin picked off the captain of the pirate ship. The men who were left, seeing that their captain had fallen, all tried to scramble into one small lifeboat and escape.

"They'll never do it!" roared the skipper. "There are too many of them."

His words came true, as the pirates, trying madly to crowd into the lifeboat, were suddenly plunged into the water as the tiny craft overturned in the rocking waves. Not a man of them ever lived to tell the tale.

"Master," cried Robin, hurriedly untying the ropes that bound him to the mast, "pull alongside the pirate vessel, and we can board her."

The skipper wasted no more time. He drew the fishing-boat alongside the great hulk of the pirate ship. As soon as the two boats touched, Robin leapt up on to the pirate ship, followed closely by the rest of the fishermen. The vessel was plainly empty.

"Let's take her back to Scarborough," cried the excited skipper. "She's a fair prize. We'll tow the fishing-boat behind."

The boat was roped to the pirate ship, and the two ships were presently sailing in the direction of the harbour. The skipper was sure of his bearings now. As the vessel glided swiftly into Scarborough harbour, the news of the coming pirate ship spread like wildfire. Soon almost the whole population were standing on the quay waiting to see this enemy ship that was pulling in so boldly. Many stood ready to repel an attack.

Directly the skipper landed, he told of the great heroism of Simon-from-over-the-Lee.

"He may not be a first-class fisherman," laughed the skipper, "but you should see his skill with the bow-and-arrows!"

The town was soon ringing with the tale. Robin was guest of honour at a feast held by the fisherfolk.

"The ship shall be yours," the skipper told Robin as soon as they were by themselves. "It was you alone who captured her."

"If I had her I should only sell her," replied Robin, honestly.

"Then sell her," said the skipper.

"I will," said Robin. "One half of the money I shall keep, and the other half I shall give to you and the crew of the fishing-boat."

He was as good as his word. When he returned to the house of the widow, he was greeted by Maid Marian. The news of his capture had spread everywhere, and Marian and the widow knew all about the exploit.

"I don't think you could keep out of trouble if you tried!" laughed Maid Marian.

Robin gave half of the money that he had as his share of the sale of the ship to the widow. She was delighted.

Robin Hood and Maid Marian stayed on in the little fishing-village. all through the winter. Then, when the buds began to burst out again on the trees, they set forth once more for their beloved home in Sherwood Forest.

CHAPTER 29

THE BLACK MONKS

ALAN-A-DALE and his wife were seated one day in the sunshine outside the hut that the outlaws had made for them. Robin had been back in the greenwood for a month now, after his stay in the fishing-village, and life in the forest went on in the old merry way.

"I feel so lazy this morning," yawned Alan-a-Dale to Ellen. "Sing to me, Ellen, and lull my mind to sleep."

Ellen laughed.

"If I sang to you it would never send you to sleep! It would be more likely to drive you away!"

They became silent again, and would not have noticed Friar Tuck walking by their dwelling if he had not greeted them in his cheery, musical voice.

"Good morning!" he called. "I am off for a walk."

He would have strolled on, but Alan-a-Dale called to him.

"Wait for us, good friar," he shouted, rising from the grass. "We will come with you."

The three walked on through the forest. They had not gone far along a leaf-strewn lane before they heard a peculiar sound.

"Quick—into these bushes!" gasped Friar Tuck.

The three dropped behind a bush. All was quiet

again. Friar Tuck raised his head above the bush, and looked about him. Not far away he could see two black horses tethered to a beech-tree.

"Strange!" he whispered, as he told Alan-a-Dale of his discovery. "Where are the owners of the horses?"

"That's something I'm going to find out!" remarked Alan-a-Dale.

"I beg your pardon!" said the friar. "You mean we!"

"All right," said Alan, with a smile. "Let us walk quietly over to the horses and see what we can find out."

They were joined by Ellen. As they neared the tethered animals, they heard a soft chanting not very far away.

It was Friar Tuck who saw the figures first. He caught hold of Alan-a-Dale's arm and halted him.

"Look!" he whispered. "Look through the trees!"

Alan and Ellen looked. Standing in a circle of birch-trees were three men in monks' habits. Two of them were black monks, the third was a mendicant friar. His gown was so dirty that Friar Tuck had difficulty in recognising the brown colour that showed him to be a friar like himself. Suddenly the three figures dropped down on their knees. The weird chanting that Friar Tuck and his friends had heard before broke the silence again.

"This is interesting," said Alan-a-Dale, softly. "Let's creep closer and listen to their chants."

The three crept silently nearer and hid themselves behind an oak-tree. They could hear the words that the monks were chanting now.

"Money, money! Send us, oh, send us some money to serve our needs!"

They sang in a low, mournful tone. The watching outlaws could clearly see the faces of the two black monks, and their expressions were sad indeed. The mendicant friar, whose back was turned to the onlookers, sang with the most unhappy voice of all. Indeed, he was having great difficulty in keeping in tune with his fellows. Altogether it was a depressing gathering.

When the dismal chant for money was over, the mendicant friar stood up and addressed the two black monks.

"My brothers," said the friar, sadly, his head shaking slowly from side to side, "we have no money. We have prayed earnestly for money to be sent us. Now our prayer is over." He hung his head in silence for a moment; then went on, with deep gloom in his low voice: "Let us search our pockets again and see what Heaven has sent us in answer to our prayers."

He looked first at one of the monks, who stood up and thrust his hands deep into the pockets of his gown.

"Alas, friar, I still have nothing!" he said.

The friar looked towards the second monk. He, too, rose and felt in his pockets. They were as empty as before.

Friar Tuck whispered to Alan-a-Dale and Ellen that the two black monks would be expected to give money to the mendicant friar if they had any on their persons. That was the custom, for mendicant friars were permitted to beg money from other people.

"It looks to me," Friar Tuck told the others in whispers, "as if the mendicant friar asked the two monks for money, and that they have been praying for some."

One of the black monks spoke again.

"As we told you before, friar, we were robbed this morning before you met us."

"It is true, O friar," said the other. "We were caught by Robin Hood's men and robbed of all our money."

"Ah, but, brothers," broke in the friar, "though you were robbed this morning, you have since prayed for money. I feel sure that your prayers have been answered."

The two black monks looked sadly at each other. They began to wonder whether the mendicant friar was a little out of his mind.

"Perhaps," went on the friar, "it would prove more fruitful if we searched each other's pockets instead of our own!"

Again the two black monks looked at each other. What a pity they had bumped into the idiotic friar that morning, they thought. Nevertheless, they obliged by searching first the friar's pockets. They soon found that he was without a penny.

"Now allow me, good monk," said the friar, as he reached out his hands towards the first monk.

Suddenly silver coins began to rain from the monk's clothing, just as if he were made of coins. Coins fairly covered the ground at his feet. The friar then searched the second monk. The same thing happened. Coins began to pour down on to the grass about his feet. Each of the monks had been wearing a belt inside his cloak, and attached to the belt were a dozen bags full of money. The friar stepped back.

"Our prayers have been answered!" he exclaimed. "We did not ask in vain. And, since we promised one another that we would share what Heaven should send, here is a handful of coins for each of you."

The two monks gaped stupidly at the wealth lying on the ground. It was all money they had saved from collections in the Abbey, and they were taking it to a safe hiding-place. But there was little that they could say to the friar, for, having once told him that they had no money on their persons, they would be proved cheats if they tried to claim the money now.

"Take your steeds," said the friar. "Go your way in the knowledge that you have done a great deed of kindness on this memorable day."

The two monks shuffled away towards where their horses were tethered.

"Oh, and by the way," called the friar after them, "next time you meet a poor man, be sure to show him as much honest charity."

The monks made no reply. They mounted their horses, and made off into the forest.

The mendicant friar stood looking after them for a few moments, then he burst out laughing. As the mounted figures vanished into the greenwood, he took off his cowl and then stepped out of his long monkish habit. Underneath he was wearing Lincoln green!

The three watchers recognised him at once. He was Robin Hood!

Suddenly Robin turned in their direction.

"Lady Ellen! Friar Tuck! Alan-a-Dale!" he cried, still laughing. "Whatever are you doing behind that tree?"

The three looked guilty. Robin Hood walked over to them.

"I saw you come," he laughed. "Did you enjoy the fun? Come and help me to pick up all this wealth."

The three ran to help their leader pick up the coins that the black monks had left behind.

"There must be well-nigh four hundred pounds here," said Friar Tuck.

Well pleased with the morning's fun, Robin Hood and his friends strode gaily back to their camp, the richer by four hundred pounds.

CHAPTER 30

THE HONEST PINDER

THE PINDER stood waiting in the field. His was a double job. He was not only responsible for seeing that all stray cattle were placed inside pounds until the owners of the beasts should call to collect them—and pay a fine for allowing them to stray—but also, as Highway Officer, for stopping people from walking across the fields when they should keep to the roads.

With his stout staff in his hand, the Pinder waited for stray cattle and stray people. He was a very honest

man. He made sure that everyone paid the correct
fine. He didn't worry whether the owner was a lord
or a peasant; the cattle never left the pound until the
fine was paid. That was how he became known as the
Honest Pinder.

Robin Hood met him when, with Will Scarlet and
Little John, the outlaw was wandering across a field
one day far from his camp. Robin and his two great
friends often used to wander far afield in search of
adventure. On this occasion they had crossed the
boundary of Nottingham and were in Wakefield, in
Yorkshire.

At the end of the field was a stile. Robin made to
clamber over it when he was stopped by a gruff voice
from the other side.

The voice was not polite.

"Where d'you think you're going, you lumbering
lout?" it said. "Don't you know the difference
between a field and a road?"

That was the Honest Pinder's way of speaking.
He was a rough, burly fellow.

Robin Hood looked at him in astonishment. He
was not used to being spoken to in that manner. He
was amused rather than annoyed.

"Do you know who I am?" he asked, genially.

"I neither know nor care!" answered the Pinder.
"I'm here to see that folk do not stray from the highway into these fields. If they do stray it is my job to
make them pay!"

Robin looked at his two companions. He could not
suppress a laugh.

"Make them pay!" he grinned. "A sound idea!
But how do you make people pay if they don't want
to?"

"I make them pay all right," retorted the Pinder.

"What if they are three to one, as we are?" asked Robin.

"I don't care if they are thirty to one!" said the Pinder stoutly. "I have a good staff in my hand, and I can crack the head of any man."

The Pinder leaned back against a tree close by the stile. He gripped his staff tightly.

Robin drew his sword and rushed at the Pinder. He was in the act of jumping the stile when his sword was suddenly swept from his hand. The Pinder had a swift eye, and he had brought his staff down on Robin's wrist at the right moment. The sword fell to the ground. Will Scarlet was next. He made a similar attempt to cross the stile with his sword raised. He met with the same treatment. Neither Robin nor he were able even to get to the Pinder's side of the stile.

Robin could not help laughing, in spite of his defeat.

"If you let us down, Little John, we are truly lost!" he said.

Little John's attempt to cross the stile was no more successful than his two friends'. His sword came crashing down to the ground at the first sweep of the Pinder's staff.

"The trouble is," said Robin, "only one of us can cross the stile at a time. Otherwise we would soon make short work of the Pinder."

Try as they might, the three friends could not overpower the Pinder, who stood his ground on the other side of the stile. Robin admired the man's pluck. He did not resent his interference, for he knew that the Honest Pinder was only doing his duty; and he had stood up to three of the strongest opponents.

At length Robin told Little John and Will Scarlet to stop trying to pass over the stile. Then he asked the Pinder what the trespass fee was. On being told, he paid him twice as much as he asked.

"How would you like a merrier job than this?" asked Robin, earnestly. "I am Robin Hood. Why not be one of my Merrie Men, and live in the greenwood with me?"

The Pinder shook his head.

"I am bound to my master for three months more," he said. "I will join you then, with pleasure."

"Oh, come, sire!" said Robin. "Come with us today and leave this uninteresting life for one of adventure."

"That is not my way," replied the honest fellow. "I have promised to stay for another three months, and stay I will. At the end of that time, as I have said, I will join you."

He was good as his word. Three months later he joined Robin Hood and his Merrie Men in Sherwood Forest. All the men respected his honesty. He soon became a very popular member.

If there was any adventure that Robin undertook, to put right a wrong, he could always rely on the Pinder's help. But if anything were planned that seemed to the Pinder unjust, then he would have nothing to do with it. Honest he was, and honest he stayed.

CHAPTER 31

A FEAST IN THE FOREST

As THE Sheriff of Nottingham had given up so much time to the capture of Robin Hood, other work that his office required him to do had fallen behind. He decided one day he must attend to this.

He was very grateful to his friend the Abbot, who offered to bring in the rents from people in some outlying districts.

The Abbot collected the rents and handed them over to a prior who was travelling with him.

"Perhaps you would be good enough to take them to the Sheriff," said the Abbott. "I have little time to spare today."

The Prior felt honoured that such an important task should be entrusted to him. He rode off through the forest with the moneybags slung round the saddle of his horse.

"What on earth are those men doing?" he asked himself, as he espied four tramps bending low over the ground. They were half hidden by bracken. "I must make some inquiries," he decided. "Hey, you fellows!" he called, trying hard to look important. "What do you think you're doing?"

The four tramps spun round. Anyone who knew them would have recognised Robin Hood, Little John, Will Scarlet, and Much-the-Miller's son.

As he came nearer, the Prior saw that a newly killed deer lay on the ground. These wretched tramps had actually killed one of the King's animals! The matter must be investigated at once!

"What is this lying in the bracken?" demanded the Prior.

"Eh?" asked Robin, feigning deafness.

"There!" shouted the Prior, pointing with his finger to the dead animal. "Down there!"

"Brown bear?" said Robin, with one hand to his ear. "No, sir; that is deer, that is."

"I know that, you fathead!" The Prior was annoyed by the simpleton. "Don't you know that deer is royal meat?"

"Boiled meat? Ah, it'll be that shortly," said Robin, innocently.

"Royal, not boiled!" shouted the Prior, bending towards Robin's ear as far as he could without falling off his horse.

"Soiled? It will be if we don't move it soon," grinned Robin, turning to his companions.

"By the heavens!" thundered the Prior. "This man must be an idiot!"

He jumped from his horse, determined to make it clear that he was not going to stand by while these four tramps carted away one of the King's deer before his very eyes.

Things did not work out as he planned, however, for he suddenly felt his arms held in grips of iron. Then he was lifted right off his feet, as Little John and Will Scarlet carried him to Robin Hood.

"I'm sorry to have caused you trouble," laughed Robin, as he threw off his tramp's disguise. "The truth is that I can't hear very well in these old clothes!"

"Robin Hood!" gasped the Prior, in terror.

"Oh, come!" smiled Robin. "We are not so bad as they say we are, you know. Come and have dinner with us, Sir Prior. Little John and Will Scarlet will hold you tightly so that you don't lose your way!"

The unhappy Prior had no option but to submit. Robin Hood and Much-the-Miller's son went on in front. The two outlaws holding the Prior walked at such a rate that at times the portly man's feet barely touched the ground.

Soon they reached the clearing in the greenwood where Robin's men were already preparing dinner. Robin sent four men to bring in the deer from where it had been left.

Dinner was a gay feast for all except one. The Prior munched his meat miserably. The venison was very good, and he secretly enjoyed it. But all those laughing eyes from the other side of the table did not make him feel much at ease. He began to wish that he had not been so forward in accepting the job of carrying the village rents to the Sheriff. The thought of all that money on the horse's saddle was disturbing. The Prior stood up as soon as the meal was over.

"Er—very nice," he blurted out—"fine food. I really must be going now!"

"Of course!" agreed Robin. "We know you must be a busy man."

"It is very kind of you," said the Prior, wondering whether he sounded as nervous as he felt. "As a matter of fact, I was saying to the Abbot yesterday . . ."

"Pardon me for interrupting," cut in Robin genially. "As you are in such a hurry, perhaps if you

F

just paid the price of your dinner we could show you a short cut to your abbey."

The Prior's face dropped. So that was it! These outlaws wanted the price of the meal he had eaten! The Prior had no doubt that the price would be high.

"I have only three shillings," he pleaded. "Surely you would not rob me of that. After all, I did not ask you for anything to eat. That was your idea."

The Prior's sound argument carried little weight with Robin.

"Then what are those moneybags slung on your horse's saddle?" asked Robin.

"That money belongs to the Sheriff!" asserted the Prior. "It represents rents from the villagers. I cannot touch it."

"I believe you," said Robin. "Now, Sir Prior, since you have only three shillings we could not ask you to pay a penny towards your dinner. You shall have it for nothing."

"Thank you, thank you!" The Prior felt greatly relieved, and some of the colour that had drained from his cheeks when Robin mentioned the moneybags began to return.

"Instead," went on Robin, with a smile, "we will accept payment from the Sheriff."

"O-oh!" wailed the Prior.

Robin turned to his men.

"Seize the moneybags!" he cried. "The Sheriff shall pay handsomely for the Prior's meal."

The moneybags were taken down from the horse's saddle, and Robin ordered a hundred pounds to be counted out and placed in one of his own bags. The Prior's moneybags were then closed and replaced on the horse, while the worthy monk stood by help-lessly.

"We're so sorry that you have to leave us," said Robin, guiding the unhappy man towards his horse. As the Prior sadly turned the horse round and started on his journey to the Sheriff, Robin called out to him: "Tell the Sheriff that Robin Hood has reduced the villagers' rents by a hundred pounds!"

"I—I daren't tell the Sheriff," said the Prior, sadly.

"Then you get your Abbot to make up the money," laughed Robin.

CHAPTER 32

ROBIN HOOD AND THE KING

THE KING of England had been told all about Robin Hood and his Merrie Men. He knew that the outlaw was a brave fighter and a fine archer. One glorious summer's day the King paid a visit to Nottingham.

"Why are all these notices promising rewards for Robin Hood's capture posted all around the town?" he asked the Sheriff of Nottingham.

"Robin Hood has defied me for many a long day, your Majesty," replied the Sheriff; "but have no fear: I shall catch him yet and bring him to justice."

"He is a great fighter and a brave man," said the King, "and he must have a warm heart. I have heard that he spends his time helping the poor."

"Yes, with money he has stolen from the rich!" pointed out the Sheriff.

The King smiled. Looking at the makeshift dishes that the Sheriff's wife had set out on the tables, the King guessed that the outlaws had not been slow in helping the poor with some of the Sheriff's property.

"I must visit Robin Hood personally," he said. "Then I can see for myself the sort of man he is."

News was quick to circulate that the King of England was planning to visit Robin Hood in the forest. He was going to take with him a hundred men.

As he was sitting dining with the Sheriff on the day before his visit, a note was brought in to him. It was from Robin Hood. It stated that if the King came to visit him with a hundred men he would never find Robin Hood. But if he chose to come alone, the outlaw would be only too pleased to make him welcome.

The King folded up the note and said nothing to the Sheriff. Later that night, however, he cancelled the order for the hundred men to accompany him the next day. He disguised himself as a monk, and set out for Sherwood Forest alone.

In the forest he saw the tall figure of a man bending over a fallen stag.

"Ho, there!" cried the King.

The man turned quickly, knife in hand.

"Is that the King's deer you have there?" asked the King.

"What if it is?" asked the tall man, who was Little John.

"Oh, nothing," replied the King.

Little John saw only a monk, who had seated himself on a log a few paces away.

"I think my master would like to see you," he said, with a grin.

He led the disguised King through the forest until they reached the outlaws' camp. Robin Hood came forward and greeted the monk.

"Welcome, Sir Monk," he said. "My men and I are having a little target practice, but we can always spare time to attend to business."

"Let me join you," suggested the monk. "I am a fair shot myself. Indeed, my friends say I am good."

"By all means join us," laughed Robin, who thought it would be a novelty to see a monk joining in the target practice.

"I see you have a noble knight amongst your band," said the monk, pointing to where a knight was preparing to aim an arrow at the target.

"He is not one of our band," Robin told him. "He is Sir Richard of Lea. I asked him to visit us today, for, to tell you the truth, we are expecting a visit from the King of England, and there is no more noble servant of the King than Sir Richard of Lea."

"Ah! Then you must be Robin Hood," said the monk. "I have heard of the King's proposed visit to you."

He was given a bow and a number of arrows, and invited to try his hand at the target. He was, to Robin's surprise, a first-class marksman.

"I'll tell you what, O monk," began Robin. "Let any who cannot hit the target receive a punch from his neighbour."

All the marksmen lined up side by side, and any who did not strike the target dead in the centre received a blow from his neighbour. When it came to the monk's turn his arrow went straight to the mark. Robin's aim was slightly off, and, since he was next to the monk, he received a hard knock from him.

"You have a strong arm," said Robin in admiration, when the shooting had ended. "Take off your cowl, good monk, and let us see you clearly."

The monk refused.

"Take it off!" Robin insisted.

Again the monk refused. Robin considered this an affront, and he smote the monk with both fists. The monk fell to the ground. Up he sprang again, however, and, striding to Robin's side, he gave the outlaw such a punching that Robin fell to the ground himself.

"You are certainly a man after my own heart," laughed Robin from the ground. "You would do well to join my band of Merrie Men."

Sir Richard of Lea came towards Robin to help him up. He turned to the monk, and then a surprising thing happened. Robin was amazed to see Sir Richard suddenly sink down upon one knee before the erect figure of the monk.

"Your Majesty!" said Sir Richard.

All the others stared in awed silence. They knew that they were standing in the presence of the King of England.

Robin was quick to kneel beside Sir Richard. All the outlaws followed suit.

"Stand, men!" ordered the King. "I have seen what manner of men you are. The stories of your bravery are true, of that I am sure. I could wish that you were in my service."

The men rose. It was an awkward moment for Robin Hood. He did not like the idea of going into the service of the King. His love was for the forest.

The King was quick to realise the reason for Robin Hood's silence.

"Well," said he, "at least I insist on you and your men escorting me along the road to Nottingham."

Two hours later the streets of Nottingham were lined with people. They had gathered there in amazement as the news spread that the King was riding towards the town at the head of Robin Hood and his Merrie Men. It was a sight they were never to forget.

When the market-place was reached, the King halted.

"Robin Hood," he announced, "I offer you a free pardon, and a free pardon for all your men, on the condition that you join my service as my valiant fighting men."

This was a great offer. Robin thought that, after all, it would be better for Maid Marian if he could settle down in the King's service. So he accepted the offer. Then he turned to his men and invited them to follow his example. Many did. Some said they would prefer to return to their homes and carry on a trade. The King agreed to allow them to do this.

When, a few days later, the King set out on his return journey to London, he was accompanied by Robin Hood, Maid Marian, and a great host of his Merrie Men.

CHAPTER 33

ROBIN HOOD AT COURT

THE MEN of Robin Hood's band who went with him to London expected to live a life of ease and plenty whilst in the King's service.

"We shall have a place to live in, plenty of food, and regular wages," they said. What more could they want?

They had not been at the King's court long before they saw how wrong they had been. When Robin applied for money to pay the wages of his men, he was told that he would be expected to pay them himself.

"All the nobles do it," explained one knight; "and so do the knights. If a man is too poor to pay his men then he has no right to be here at all!"

Robin had brought with him a tremendous chest filled with gold coins. He was able to pay his men their proper wages from it. Yet he knew that the gold would not last for ever. He soon learnt that few of the knights paid their men anything at all.

Robin was light-hearted and happy at first. He paid his men their wages, and was free with his money. Other knights took advantage of his happy-go-lucky spirit to borrow from him.

"Robin Hood," one would say, "I am short of money. I want to pay my men, who are beginning to grumble. I beg you to lend me enough to pay them, or there will be trouble amongst them."

Robin always was kind-hearted. He knew, also, that there might come a day when he would need the friendship of the knights. So he gave them money from his chest.

"I'm beginning to see the wood at the bottom of the chest," he murmured to himself one day. "It will not be long before the chest is empty."

His words came true. There came a day when he had no money left. Now would be his chance, he thought, to borrow back from the many knights who had so long been borrowing from him. He asked some of them to repay their debts. None could. Knights who were once his best friends now spurned him. With money, Robin found that everyone was his friend. Without it only his old comrades stood loyally by him.

He called all his men to him, and told them honestly of the state of affairs. They were sympathetic, but they could not live without pay, and before long most of them left the court and returned to their homes. Once there, they found the attraction of their old forest habits too strong for them, and they lived once more under the greenwood trees.

Robin Hood bore the life at court as long as he could. Few friends were with him now. He was lonely. He talked to Maid Marian of his great urge to return to Sherwood Forest. Marian knew that he would never be happy away from his beloved greenwood, so she said that she was willing to return to the forest with him.

"You must first ask the King, Robin," she said. "He would never forgive you if you left without his permission."

"I will," agreed Robin.

He sought permission from the King's Chamberlain to see the King. When he was at last admitted to the royal presence, he told of the hunger in his heart to see the greenwood once more.

"It is a kind of homesickness, sire," said Robin. "Until I have again seen my greenwood home, and until I have stayed there for a time, I'm sure I shall not be able to settle down to anything."

The King considered Robin's plea.

"H'm!" he murmured, after a short silence. "I think there is something in what you say, Robin Hood." He was a just man and he knew that Robin would be of little use to him in his present state of mind. A refreshing holiday in his greenwood home might work wonders. "I will grant you your wish," he said at length. "You may visit Sherwood Forest again; but you must return to me in two weeks' time. Not a day longer than that must you stay."

Robin left the King's room in a happy frame of mind. He ran straight to Maid Marian and told her the good news. He left for Sherwood Forest that day, arranging for Maid Marian to follow a week later by horse and wagon. She could never have undertaken the journey on foot, and Robin found that no one could be persuaded to start out in less than a week. Thus he set out alone on the long journey.

CHAPTER 34

ROBIN'S HOMECOMING

MUCH-THE-MILLER'S son was now in charge of his mill, for his father had died and left him the mill. He was out of touch with the outlaws who had not gone with Robin Hood to London. His only link with the happy past was Friar Tuck.

Every Sunday, Friar Tuck and he would meet and stroll into the greenwood.

On one of these walks, when both were feeling a little sad, Much-the-Miller's son turned suddenly to the friar.

"Did you hear a sound?" he asked, excitedly.

"No," said Friar Tuck. "What sound was it?"

"Perhaps it was nothing."

"I have heard that some of the folk are back in the forest," said Friar Tuck.

"What sort of folk do you mean?"

"Our sort," said the Friar. He corrected himself. "I mean, the sinful sort we once were."

"There it is again," said the other, interrupting him.

There was no doubt about the noise this time. It was the old call of the horn that once they knew so well.

The two ran in the direction of the sound. What they would meet they knew not. They hoped desperately that, by some amazing stroke of good fortune, they would meet their old master again.

Soon they came to a small opening amongst the trees, where three men were grouped. One of them was bending over another, who was lying on the ground. He appeared to be exhausted. The third was a giant in size. As soon as he saw Much-the-Miller's son and Friar Tuck coming towards him he drew a knife from his belt.

Friar Tuck recognised the man at once.

"Put away your knife, Little John," he called. "Do you not remember us? We are your old companions, Friar Tuck and Much-the-Miller's son."

Little John was happy indeed to see his old friends once more.

"Who's with you?" asked the friar.

"The one bending down," said Little John, "is Will Scarlet. Surely he has not so changed that you fail to recognise him?"

"And who is that on the ground?" asked Much-the-Miller's son as they walked nearer to the figure.

"The captain!" whispered Will Scarlet, turning from the prostrate form of Robin.

Friar Tuck ran forward to his old master.

"Robin! Sweet Robin!" he cried. "Look up, my master! You remember your old chaplain!"

Robin pulled himself up. After walking all the way from London, with hardly a scrap to eat, he was weak and almost worn out. It had been a hard, four-days journey. He would never have completed it if he had not been so determined to see the friendly forest once again. Now that he was back in the greenwood he knew that he would soon recover.

"It is grand to see you," he said to Friar Tuck

and Much-the-Miller's son. "I have been given only fourteen days' leave from the King to visit my forest haunts, and the days will soon pass, I fear."

With a sudden effort, Robin stood on his feet. He placed his horn to his lips. The old familiar call rang out through the forest. Figures streaked through the greenwood towards them. Presently a crowd of Robin's old outlaws were gathered round him once more.

Robin put away his horn, and looked happily at his old comrades. Already he felt his old gaiety and joy of life returning. Many of the outlaws facing him, he noticed, had joined him when he left Nottingham to serve the King; but one by one they had left the King's service to go back to Sherwood Forest. This was the life they knew and loved; this was where their hearts were.

"Welcome! Welcome, my old friends!" cried Robin. "I have come again to shoot the King's deer —but only for a short time."

Little John and Will Scarlet sat together that evening. Robin Hood had gone to bed early, for he was still very tired.

"Our master must stay with us," said Little John. "He needs us just as much as we need him."

"He will never go back on his word to the King," said Will Scarlet.

"But if he were held here by force he would not be able to keep his promise, would he?" grinned Little John.

"What do you mean?"

"Supposing you and I bound him and held him prisoner! He couldn't possibly return."

Little John was in earnest. He knew where his

master's heart lay. He knew also that it would only
be by force that Robin would be persuaded to stay
in his forest home, instead of obeying the King's
command to return after fourteen days.

Together Little John and Will Scarlet worked out
a plan to capture Robin and hold him captive until
one of them had visited the King and explained how
dear to Robin Hood was his life in the forest.

The plan was complete by the time Robin was due
to start back on his long journey to London. Maid
Marian had joined him some days before, and she
had been told by Little John of what was afoot. She
kept silent about it until the day of Robin's departure.

As he was making ready to leave the camp, Little
John and Will Scarlet pounced on him from behind.
Robin was unprepared, and could not understand the
meaning of the outrage. He was even more mystified
when he found himself tightly secured with stout
ropes.

Little John stepped in front of him.

"Forgive us, master," he said apologetically. "We
know that you will not stay of your own free will.
We know, too, that your heart lies here in the greenwood. So we are holding you captive until a messenger returns from the King to tell us his views."

Robin was furious at the trick that had been played
on him; but he was powerless to act.

Will Scarlet left that day for London. He was
gone a week. On his return from the King of England, he called Little John to him, and together they
reported to Robin.

"Master," said Will, smiling, "I explained to the
King that you were held captive by your own men.
I told him that this was your true home and that you

could never be happy at Court. I begged him to allow you to stay here with us. The King listened to all I had to say. Then, after a long silence, he replied that you could stay in Sherwood Forest on condition that you and all the Merrie Men would be at his service, if ever the country was in danger. I gave him that assurance."

"You mean, I am free to stay?" asked Robin, incredulously.

"Yes, master," answered Will Scarlet joyfully. "Let us live again the life of adventure that we once loved so well."

Robin was overjoyed at the news. So was Little John. All the outlaws in the forest were summoned to the camp, and they made a great feast under the trees to celebrate Robin Hood's return to the old life of freedom and adventure in the greenwood.

CHAPTER 35

SWORD-FIGHT TO FREEDOM

DURING Robin Hood's absence from the greenwood, a new Sheriff had been elected at Nottingham.

Robin soon learned the ways of the new man. He was not at all like the former Sheriff, against whom Robin had long battled his wits.

This new Sheriff was a weak man, who did little to interfere with anything that was carried out, whether right or wrong. He wanted to live and let live without causing any disturbance to the peace of Nottingham. On the only occasion that he came face to face with Robin he ran for his life! It happened in this way.

The Sheriff's finest swordsman determined to capture Robin Hood. He persuaded the Sheriff to go to Sherwood Forest with him. He succeeded in capturing Little John. Ordering him to be bound to a tree, the Sheriff told the swordsman to go deeper into the forest in search of Robin Hood, he himself staying behind to keep guard over Little John.

The swordsman covered his armour with a horse-skin. This gave him the appearance of a poor vagabond.

He travelled deep into the forest, but found no sign of Robin. Dismounting, he sat under a tree. Presently two of Robin's men came along. They appeared to be carrying a deer between them.

The swordsman decided to follow the two men. They would surely lead him to their master.

Stealthily, using all the cunning and woodcraft that he knew, he shadowed the men. They gave no sign of having seen him, and he was satisfied that he was unobserved.

Actually the two men were fully aware that they were being followed. At first they suspected that the man in the strange horse-hide costume was bent on stealing their deer, so they decided to let him follow them until he came up and tried to wrest the deer from them. Yet nothing happened. He just dogged them steadily through the forest.

Suddenly one of the men realised the true purpose of the pursuer. He wanted them to lead him to Robin Hood.

He whispered to his companion. The fellow should have his money's worth! It would be an easy matter to make short work of him once they decoyed him to the outlaws' lair.

Before long they came to the camp. Robin Hood was sitting on a log under a tree, testing his bow. Swiftly, the men warned him that they had been followed all the way through the forest by the stranger.

Robin jumped to his feet and blew his horn. From out of the trees dashed men from his newly formed band. The numbers grew, and the swordsman was swiftly surrounded, and his way of escape cut off. A great host of men closed him in. Robin Hood's band of Merrie Men was as strong now as it had ever been.

The swordsman looked round in alarm. Then, seeing that he could not escape, he went straight to Robin Hood and flung off his horse-hide covering. Robin recognised him as a soldier of the Sheriff.

"Welcome!" said Robin, bowing mockingly.

"Robin Hood!" said the swordsman. "I have sworn to the Sheriff of Nottingham to take you back with me. Little John is captured, and is bound to a tree not two miles from here. You are a man of valour, 'tis said, and as such you will not shrink from fair fight."

This was a direct challenge to Robin.

"There is nothing I would love more," he made answer. "Choose your weapons."

The Sheriff's man was one of the most brilliant swordsmen in the country. Robin knew this, and he knew that the man would at once choose his favourite weapon, the sword. He did.

The combat began. As the two figures fought, the circle of outlaws closed round them. The men cheered their leader on, but Robin needed no encouragement. This was his first fight since his return to the forest. It would prove his mettle once again, or it would end in death at the hand of the Sheriff's swordsman.

· Robin fought with great skill. His thrusts and parries were quicker than those of his foe, but the man was a master of the art, and he fought ruthlessly and fiercely. He knew that his life depended on it. At length, however, he started to tire. He was much older than Robin Hood. The outlaw saw his chance. He pressed his opponent harder than ever. Slowly he wore him down. The ring of steel upon steel rang out through the forest.

Suddenly, with a savage thrust, Robin struck his opponent in an unguarded moment. The swordsman fell with a groan, never to rise again.

The cheers that greeted Robin's victory echoed through the forest. Robin ordered the swordsman's clothes to be taken from him, and the corpse buried. This done, Robin dressed in the slain man's attire and set out to find Little John, first learning from the two men who had carried in the deer the direction in which to go.

Presently he came upon Little John, who was still tied to a tree, with the Sheriff of Nottingham standing guard over him. The Sheriff looked relieved when he saw Robin, believing him to be his swordsman.

"Ho, there, Sheriff!" called Robin. "Robin Hood is slain. Allow me to loosen the bonds of this varlet so that we can take him for public hanging in Nottingham."

So saying, Robin untied Little John, whispering to the giant as he did so who he was.

When he had freed Little John, Robin threw off the swordsman's clothing, revealing his suit of Lincoln green.

The Sheriff was too terrified to move. He stood aghast, staring at the two outlaws.

"Ha, ha, Little John!" laughed Robin. "What do you think of a Sheriff of Nottingham who cannot move himself backwards or forwards?"

He strode up to the Sheriff and said: "Go, good Sheriff, for I have no wish to harm you; only never venture into the forest alone, lest Robin Hood bite you!"

The Sheriff needed no urging. He turned and ran to where his horse was standing. In the space of seconds, he was scuttling away towards Nottingham.

Laughing heartily, Robin and Little John linked arms, and strolled through the greenwood.

CHAPTER 36

CLEMENT OF THE GLEN

CLEMENT OF THE GLEN was the nickname given to one of Robin's outlaws. He was a married man, but he had not seen his wife for a long time. There had been trouble in the village where he lived, and his only chance of escape had been to vanish into the forest to join Robin Hood and his band.

"If only I could see my wife once again," he would say to himself sometimes when he was sitting alone in his forest home, "I should feel at peace."

He was determined to seek out his wife again at the first opportunity. The chance, however, did not arise, and he spoke about his troubles to Robin one day.

"If opportunity does not come to you," advised Robin, "you must make the opportunity yourself."

Clement of the Glen thought deeply about the advice that his master had given. He would make his own opportunity that very day!

Off he set through the forest, along the Nottingham road, through the city, and to a village on the other side.

He came at last to his cottage. His wife was happy indeed when she saw him coming along the road, and she ran to meet him. They linked arms and went into the house.

"I've had to take in a lodger," she told him. "She is an old lady and seldom goes out; but she pays generously for her room, and I am able to live on the money she pays me."

Clement of the Glen noticed the old lady sitting on a stool in the darkened kitchen; but he had thoughts only for his wife. The old lady was offended that this man should pass her by without even a greeting.

She knew something of the circumstances that had sent Clement of the Glen away from his home to join Robin Hood's band. With a feeling of resentment at what she thought was a slight, she went from the cottage in search of one of the Sheriff's men.

"Clement of the Glen is back!" she said, when she

met the Sheriff's man along the road. "He's in the cottage now!"

The old lady may have regretted her hasty action later, but she acted under the urge of her resentment. She kept away from the cottage, for she knew that action would soon follow.

In less than an hour a strong party of the Sheriff's men bore down upon the cottage.

Clement of the Glen was happily telling tales of his forest life to his wife. Suddenly he heard the sound of horses' hooves along the road. He looked out of the doorway, then quickly darted back to where his wife was sitting.

"The Sheriff's men are here!" he exclaimed. "We must not let them in!"

Together they placed furniture against the bolted door, and awaited the coming of the riders. Clement stood ready behind the door, with his longbow in his hand. His wife grasped a chopper, determined to do what damage she could to the attackers.

The Sheriff's men, unable to get in, tried to break down the door, then through the splintered wood they saw the two brave figures, Clement and his wife, one poising a bow-and-arrow, the other holding a chopper.

The Sheriff's men were checked. They saw at once that whoever first approached would lose his life. They would have to think out a plan if they were to capture Clement of the Glen that day without casualties to themselves.

"Burn the place down!" cried the leader of the men suddenly.

It was not long before flames began to leap along the front of the cottage.

"The scoundrels!" cried Clement.

He raced to the back of the cottage. Looking out of the window, he found that the fire had not reached this part.

"Come here!" he cried to his wife. "Come quickly! Jump out of the window! Run for your life into the forest! I will join you later."

Clement helped his wife to drop to the ground from the window. She begged him to hurry. He disappeared again into the room, where the smashed door was now alight. He could see through the flames that a large crowd had gathered. Angry fists were shaken at him.

"Come out and take your punishment!" sneered the leader of the Sheriff's men.

Clement's answer was to send a steady stream of arrows through the burning doorway. He kept this up until the intense heat from the flames forced him to throw down his bow. Snatching his sword from its hook on the wall, he dashed through the flaming doorway into the midst of the Sheriff's men, waving the sword left and right.

"Get him, men!" cried the leader. "Get him before he kills anyone else."

The suddenness of Clement's attack, however, made them all give before him. He dashed through the mob and ran along the road. His only chance of escape was down an alley that opened out from the street. He dashed into it; but the Sheriff's men gave chase. Clement turned to face them, fighting savagely, slashing his sword to right and left in a last fierce bid for freedom.

He went down fighting. The Sheriff's men overwhelmed him. In a short time he was tied from head to foot, and dragged back to the road, where the leader of the men was standing.

"Fling him into prison!" ordered the leader.

In his prison, Clement of the Glen knew that this was the end for him. It was comforting to know that his wife was free. As he lay on the rush-covered floor, he heard the continual tap-tap of the hammers outside his cell. They were building the scaffold. The Sheriff did not waste much time!

Meanwhile, a lad from the town had run into the forest directly he heard of Clement's capture. Clement had many times helped this lad, and now a chance had come to repay him.

It was Robin Hood himself who first saw the lad in the forest. He hailed him.

"It's Clement of the Glen, sir," said the lad. "He's been captured and is now in prison. They are going to hang him, sir."

Robin was quick to act. He took Little John with him at once to Nottingham. Coming to the prison entrance, the two knocked on the door and waited.

"What d'you want?" demanded a surly voice. A man opened the door four or five inches to examine the visitors.

Robin's fist crashed home on the man's jaw before he had finished his sentence. They were in! Little John snatched up the porter's keys as the two rushed to Clement's cell.

"It's easy to tell which is Clement's cell," laughed Robin. "Hear the din he is making!"

In quick time Robin and Little John had opened Clement's cell, and were set for freedom, but they suddenly saw the Sheriff himself coming towards them.

The three outlaws stopped in their tracks.

"This is the opportunity I have been waiting for!" sneered the Sheriff. "You are trapped in my own prison, too, which will save us much trouble!"

He leaned against the scaffold that had been erected during the night.

Suddenly an arrow sang through the air. Robin had taken lightning aim. The arrow pierced the Sheriff's coat, and held him pinned to the scaffold.

"Confound you!" he bellowed, struggling to free himself. "Help! Help!"

His cries were soon answered, but not soon enough to catch the escaping outlaws. They sped on and were nearing the outskirts of Nottingham by the time the chase had really been organised.

Bursting into the forest, they came upon a woman. She was weeping. Clement of the Glen recognised her at once.

"She is my wife," he cried in delight.

That day another member was added to Robin Hood's band, for Clement's wife joined them in the forest and made her home there. She was made welcome by Maid Marian, and she soon learned to love the ways of the greenwood and the friendliness of its inhabitants.

CHAPTER 37

THE DEATH OF ROBIN HOOD

ROBIN HOOD lived for many more years under the greenwood trees. Most of his original band had come back to the forest after their leader's return from service with the King of England. As the years went by, many of them passed peacefully away and were buried under the leafy carpet that was their home.

Though he was grey-haired now, Little John remained with Robin until the end. Maid Marian, who had grown old with Robin, and who had ever been content to share with him the life that they both loved, joined a nunnery. Robin wanted her to do this before she died, for he knew that the life of the outlaws was hard, and that Sherwood Forest was no home for aged people.

One spring morning Robin Hood awoke and called Little John to his side.

"I am old, Little John," he said. "Before I die I want once more to see Maid Marian."

"The Kirke Hall Priory is far from here, master," said Little John.

"We can reach it somehow, Little John," said Robin. "Why, in the old days we would think nothing of the distance."

"We were young then," sighed Little John.

However, the two men set out through the greenwood toward the priory where Maid Marian had gone less than a year before. Maid Marian was no longer alive. She had missed Robin and the free life of the greenwood. She lived only three months after her entry into the priory.

It was drawing towards early evening when the two men reached the postern door of the priory.

"Ring the bell, Little John," said Robin.

Little John did so. There was a muffled clanging from within.

Presently the Prioress came to the door and greeted them. Robin told her that he wished to see Maid Marian. The Prioress invited them inside. Little John sat on a rugged wooden seat outside the priory to await the return of his master. By his side were his longbow and his arrows. Robin's bow and arrows were lying at his feet.

When Robin learned that Maid Marian was no longer alive he was overcome with grief.

"Take me to her room," he pleaded softly, "that I may see where she spent her last days."

The Prioress led him up a flight of stone stairs to the room where Maid Marian had been living. Robin walked to the window. He was weak now. He knew that his own end was near. Beyond the window lay the greenwood, quiet and still. Robin raised his horn once again to his lips.

Little John heard the three faint blasts. Their very faintness told him that something was wrong with his old master. He sprang up and rushed into the building.

"He is in here," called the Prioress. "I think he needs you."

Little John rushed up the staircase and joined his master.

"Little John," cried Robin, weakly, "I am dying. Give me once more my bow in my hand that I may shoot an arrow through the window. Where it falls, there shall you have me buried."

Little John was back shortly with Robin's bow and an arrow. He raised his master to the level of the window, and with one final effort Robin sent his last arrow speeding through the casement. All his great strength seemed to come to him for that one shot. Swift and true, the arrow flew on its way, far into the forest that had been Robin Hood's home. Contented, Robin fell back into the arms of Little John.

"That was a long shot, Little John."

In silence the two old friends gazed towards the greenwood.

"When you have laid me down, Little John," said Robin, "and I am gone, search for my arrow, and where it has fallen bury me there beneath the sward."

So Robin was buried, as he had wished, by Little John where his last arrow had come to rest.

So passed Robin Hood, the gay outlaw; but the memory of his adventures lives on, and will live on, forever.